# DARK MAGI

## A REPUBLIC CHRONICLES
## PREQUEL

JOANNA WHITE

# JOANNA WHITE

# Dark Magi

Cover by: GetCovers
First edition November 2019
Second edition November 2022
ISBN 9781697478532

# DARK MAGI

## OTHER BOOKS BY JOANNA WHITE

# JOANNA WHITE

## ACKNOWLEDGEMENTS

To my family for their support and my husband for his help fixing this story to make it what it is today. To Vibrant Designs for the beautiful, free cover. To Alex and Kyra and all your help in breaking this story apart to rebuild it and make it the book it is today.

I also want to give a special thanks to Ariel Paiement, Several7s, JesterheadJohnSnow, and CCWinters for being my writer friends on wattpad.com, for your amazing characters and your permission to use them, and their fun journey they took with Kyren and I. You guys are amazing writers and have changed my life for the better.

But especially thanks to Jesus Christ, my Lord and Savior and my Heavenly Father, who writes these stories with me and gives me the passion for writing and storytelling.

# DARK MAGI

## CONTENTS

# JOANNA WHITE

# CHAPTER ONE

PAIN.

IT RIPPLED through Kyren's back, tearing apart flesh, ripping through bone and sinew with every strike. The makeshift whip slashed at him again and again, never wavering as it licked his skin, bringing agony to every inch that it kissed.

Kyren clenched his jaw so tightly his teeth ached, but he refused to cry out.

"Next time, bring the supplies to the kitchens not the pantries!" The overseer, a fat, balding man who sat upon his stool, talked with his mouth full. He was munching away at a leg of a *Druzhr*—a creature with a leg so thick it could have fed Kyren's wife and two children for a week or two. The overseer gestured to the guards, who pulled the *Assel* away. It was a beast of an animal—the only thing in the castle fatter than the overseer, Kyren suspected. They were larger than horses with a single horn protruding from the center of the beast's head, and two long tentacle-like trunks hung on either side in place of ears. *Assels* were trained to use their tentacles as whips, and they brought severe pain and tissue damage with every strike. He would know—he had been flogged by them many times.

The guards unchained him from the whipping post and threw him down. Kyren collapsed onto the ground, his entire back numb. The offense was a lie. They *had* told him to bring the supplies to the pantries. He had no doubt his mother had been annoyed with him and made up the excuse so she could enjoy watching him being whipped.

His mother strolled toward the gardens with the other High Noblewomen of Komesten. As they passed, they stopped mid-giggle when they stared at his bloodied body. Many of the women grimaced and frowned, as if he was a stray dog that needed to be killed and thrown into a ditch. It reminded him of what his wife used to say about his mother and how she treated him.

*"Kyren," Ashyra murmured, placing a hand upon his arm.*

*Kyren stared after his mother as she strode down the hallway, body trembling as his fists clenched. "You can't help me, Ashyra. So stop trying."*

*Ashyra shook her head and then used her hands to yank his face to look down at her. "No." Her lip jutted out stubbornly just like it always did. "I refuse to give up on you, Kyren Asherex."*

*"Why don't you hate me? Everyone else does."*

*Ashyra placed a finger to his lips. "Kyren, I care about you because you're different. How many slaves have you helped since you've become one yourself? Your mother doesn't mean what she says…"*

Now, in the present moment, as the memory faded from his mind and Kyren looked up and met his mother's eyes as he trembled helplessly beneath her, Vassti reached out her hands and used her magic to pry into his mind. He grunted, but his weakened body kept him from fighting her as much as he normally did.

*No,* he mentally begged, but that only made her press him further.

She took the memory of Ashyra, twisted it. Kyren knew it wasn't real, but it still stung. *"I hate you,"* Vassti whispered in his mind through the image of Ashyra. *"You mean nothing to me. You never should have been born, Kyren."*

Vassti laughed sadistically and backed away, joining her friends as they left him behind.

# DARK MAGI

Kyren closed his eyes, feeling tears burning there and he tried recall the rest of the real memory to help remind himself that Ashyra loved him.

Did she?

*You never should have been born.*

*Kyren felt tears burning his eyes and crying in front of Ashyra was the last thing he wanted. He stared at the empty place in the hallway where his mother had just told him how that he was worthless and that seeing him alive and well made her sick.*

*All his life, he had tried to please both his parents, but it had never been enough. No,* he *had never been enough, not for anyone.*

*"You're enough for me," Ashyra whispered. He realized he had spoken the words out loud. In that moment, Kyren loved her more than anyone. She loved him when he felt unloveable, when no one else cared, when his own mother wanted him to die. It was Ashyra who cared for him. Being loved and cared for meant more than he realized; he had never had it before, so it was foreign to him.*

A sharp kick to his side snapped Kyren awake. He hadn't even realized he had fallen unconscious. Desperately, he clung to the returned memory and tried to forget the image his mother had planted inside his thoughts.

Another kick finally made Kyren glance up.

"You're being summoned to the palace, slave," a messenger snapped.

Kyren eyed the scrawny kid with a glare that could cut through glass. Ten years ago, he would have had the boy beaten for that tone.

Now he was the one being beaten. *Serves you right,* Kyren thought. He gritted his teeth as he hurried toward the staircase, bringing fresh pain to his back. The distance between the bitter prince he had once been and the man he was today was all because of Ashyra. She loved him and saw more in him than anyone ever had.

Instead of following the staircase up, toward the royal court, he headed down a small hallway for servants and slaves. After winding his way around, he finally arrived at the slave bathhouse. The numbness slowly started fleeing and as Kyren stumbled into the room, he placed his hands on the walls on either side of him to steady himself. The tiny space left little room for him to fit inside. The floor, ceiling, and walls were all made entirely from gray stone, and the ceiling was so low, Kyren had to crouch down.

# DARK MAGI

Pain flared in his back, and this time, Kyren grunted. He had so many scars on his back, it protected him from most of the fresh whippings he received, but nothing would help take away the pain or the shame.

The hot water stung his back, bringing unshed tears to his eyes. He washed quickly, and dried off, groaning as the cloth tore at his mutilated skin. Collapsing onto the floor, he panted, trying to push the pain back.

He thought about going to the Temple to worship the Father but questioned whether it would help him at all. Ashyra told him that prayers solved every problem. He had never grown up believing in the Holy Creator or His Son, but Ashyra had brought him to the Father's Light in more ways than one. She was a prayer warrior. It was she who had prayed that his father leave their children be and it was she who had prayed for Kyren's redemption.

Now, as he debated, the pain flaring in his back made the decision for him. The Temple was simply too far away. In any case, he was due in court. Couldn't he simply pray here? He wasn't very good at this.

"Father… Creator… You know how unnatural this is for me." Kyren pushed himself to his knees with a grunt. "To be honest, I don't even know what I'm praying about..." He paused, but all he could focus on was the pain in his back and he lost whatever words he had been about to say.

"Kyren?"

At the sound of his uncle's voice, he used the wall to push himself up. "Uncle Jahad," Kyren said. Did he really sound so breathless?

Frowning, Jahad turned him around, and then sucked in a sharp breath. "Again? Kyren that's—"

"You know me, Jahad. I've been a naughty boy." Kyren would have smirked, but he didn't have the energy.

As he turned back around, Jahad shook his head, looking as if he wanted to smack him. Kyren was thankful his uncle chose not to. "Your father is getting impatient," Jahad said instead.

Kyren nodded and followed Jahad, slipping a shirt over his head as they left the bathhouse. Jahad took a shortcut outside and across the grassy yard, heading into a room that led to the private dining hall. After making a sharp turn and taking the staircase two stairs at a time, Jahad shoved open the doors to Vaxon's throne room. Kyren followed much more slowly, but eventually caught up to his uncle.

# DARK MAGI

They had entered through the back way, coming from a side hallway halfway to the throne.

Jahad inclined his head to his brother, who sat on the throne at the back of the room.

"Leave us." At the king's command, Jahad left the room.

Kyren didn't bother to bow or incline his head. Instead, he crossed his arms and glared at his father. He was a bulk of a man, standing taller than Kyren by several inches. His black hair was graying in places, but the cruelness of his eyes did not waver and nothing about him showed his age.

"What do you want?" When it came to his father, it was always best to come straight to the point. Vaxon hated waiting, and he definitely hated those pompous wretches who beat around the bush. Instead of answering, he gestured.

From a hallway in the back, four Nires guards stomped out. Four humanoid lizards, standing at seven to eight feet tall, strode into the room on two feet instead of four. Their scales were magic-resistant, which meant Kyren wouldn't be able to fight them. The Nires held his wife Ashyra, a short young woman with black curls that hung around her in beautiful ringlets. Her blue eyes were bloodshot from tears. They met Kyren's in desperation and fear. "Kyren!" she screamed.

He'd met her three years ago after one of Vaxon's torture sessions. Vaxon liked to casually force Kyren's mind back to a memory of being tortured.

*His legs gave way, even though he knew he wasn't really tied on the rack.*

*"Are you okay?" A woman bent down and placed her hands on either side of him. "Do I need to help you to the slave quarters?"*

*Kyren shook his head and stumbled to his feet. It felt as if his legs were being torn apart... He swallowed back a scream and his eyes watered.*

*The woman smiled gently at him, grabbed the boxes he had been carrying, and slung her arm around his waist. "Let me help you."*

*When they reached a corridor away from the other guards, Kyren glanced at her. She was beautiful, for a handmaiden. Long black ringlets curled around her shoulders and her warm, blue eyes smiled at him as well as her kindhearted expression did. "What's your name?"*

*"Ashyra. Yours?"*

*"Kyren."*

*She gasped. "The prince?"*

*"Ex-prince," he muttered bitterly.*

# DARK MAGI

*She never asked him questions and was the first person to not look at him with disgust or disdain.*

Now, he had to help her. Somehow, someway, he couldn't let this happen. Just as Kyren took a step toward her, a Nires holding her pressed a claw to her throat. Another one yanked the tiny arm of his two year old son. "Papa!" the boy cried.

The last Nires held his three-week old infant daughter.

His breathing froze, his thoughts blanked out. Something inside him snapped. A part of himself he had forced back for nearly ten years, resurfaced in the blink of an eye. The heavy sensation pulsed and oozed through his veins, burning everything it came in contact with. Energy surged inside him in a wild burst and he longed to feel the darkness in his hands again. Despite the anti-magic collar around his neck, he could feel power thudding inside him again. The temptation to attack his father was so strong that only the anti-magic collar kept him from it.

"Let them go." Three words. Three simple words, and yet... they were so much more. As he glared at his father, those words defied him. Kyren cursed him in his heart and hated him with a blackened passion.

# JOANNA WHITE

"Oh, I will let them live." Vaxon stood, saying a new word each time he took a step down from the dais. "But only if you do something for me first."

*Before I can even get to the guards to take them out, Vaxon will stop me. Even if I did get to the Nires, there's nothing I can do against them. And if I take time to fight Vaxon, the guards will kill them,* Kyren thought. Every logical point of escape was blocked, and he mentally cursed. He was trapped with no way around whatever was about to happen.

Vaxon gestured, and the Nires guards left the room, dragging his wife and children with them.

"What do you want me to do?" Kyren's let his tone become as dark as his father's. Void of sarcasm, it left no room for idle chatter.

"You're going to be thrown into the arena with those rogue Magi scum who foolishly thought they could fight against me. You will make sure that every single one of them dies. Do you understand?" Vaxon's ice-cold blue eyes met Kyren's with a glare that weighed a thousand pounds. Anyone else would have buckled but Kyren had lived beneath that gaze all his life.

# DARK MAGI

"I'll kill whoever you want. But what makes me think you'll keep your word?"

Vaxon cocked his head and paced in a circle around Kyren. "Whatever do you mean, son?"

Kyren flinched at the word. "Face it, *Father,* if you're throwing me in the arena, there's only one reason. You want me dead. You can come up with a thousand different ways to kill the rebel Magi prisoners. Why use me?"

Vaxon shrugged. "I love the twist of irony of those children dying by a hand of a friend."

Kyren glared at the floor. For the first time in the entire conversation, Vaxon hit a nerve. *He never wanted me, even before I joined the rebellion against him.*

"You wish to know why I would let your wife and children live after you die? It's simple, really. Your wife, Ashyra, is a very important person... More than just a mere servant. Her parents sit upon the *Xandai* throne. We need their alliance and our trades with them in silk and mammoth tusks," Vaxon explained.

The fact that Vaxon had discovered Ashyra's secret came as no surprise. He had eyes and ears everywhere, and if he didn't already know something, he soon found out.

# JOANNA WHITE

*If he knows about her, then it's true—she has been brought to the palace as a prisoner. A hostage to ensure Xandai's loyalty,* Kyren thought. It also explained why Vaxon had spared Ren after he had found out about their secret marriage and why he allowed them to have Rya.

Kyren felt no relief at the news; if Ashyra was important enough to Vaxon for him to keep her alive after his death, his father still wouldn't hesitate to kill her and their children the moment he disobeyed.

He had no choice.

"When do I get started?" Kyren sighed.

Vaxon smiled. "I was hoping you would ask."

**DARK MAGI**

# CHAPTER TWO

OVER THE COURSE of the next several weeks, Vaxon used his spies, as well as Kyren's old contacts and Queen Vassti's magic to track down the last of the Magi who had chosen to rebel against his reign; a total of thirty-two of them. Two powerful Magi who had the power of light, called Light Mages, were believed to have been dead, but it was soon discovered that they were still alive.

They were powerful twins and even though Vaxon wanted to capture them to ensure the job was done right, but because they were Light Mages, their magic would cancel out both Kyren and even Vaxon's darkness. So if they attacked them outright, it would be a pointless fight.

For that reason, Vaxon sent Kyren to them, alone, acting as if he had escaped his father and wished to join them. How Kyren wished it were true. They quickly believed him, to Kyren's dismay. On his father's orders, he used poisons to knock them out and capture them.

Two days later, Vaxon ordered Kyren to accompany him to attack a large group of Magi who had chosen to stay together. "Wouldn't some of the Magi tried to use the spaceships to escape off planet?" Kyren asked, just before he and his father left.

Vaxon shook his head. "No. I disabled all of the magic on the ships long before this rebellion for that reason."

Kyren gasped. "You did it when you took the throne from—"

Vaxon snarled at him. "Don't say that name. I took the throne from that scum that the Republic put on the throne and he's gone forever. You and the other Magi who rebelled against me will all pay. The Republic, the Magi Order... None of them can help. All the rebellious Magi left on Castre will die, including you, Kyren. There is no escaping the planet, not for any of you."

Kyren shook his head, feeling a pang of sorrow in his chest. "I would never try to escape. I wouldn't leave my family."

Vaxon threw his head back and laughed. "Of course you wouldn't. At least you're not a coward. That's one good thing about you in a sea of reasons of why I hate you."

The words stung, but Kyren kept his face impassive. He refused to show his father how much it hurt him. That would only bring his father more enjoyment, being the sadistic monster that he was.

The thought that the Republic and the Magi Order couldn't help them made Kyren even less hopeful. Vaxon had taken the throne, murdered the King and his entire household, subjugated the people, and the Republic had no idea what was going on. Castre was an isolated planet, far away from Republic space, so without anyone on Castre being able to escape the planet, then the Republic would never know what was happening.

Once Vaxon finished off the Magi on Castre, Kyren had no doubt that he would try to bring down both the Magi Order and the Republic. With both capital planets being so far away, they wouldn't see him coming until it was too late.

Vaxon's spies had learned the location of the camp where the Magi fled, so Vaxon used darkness to teleport Kyren and himself there. Vaxon wrapped darkness around Kyren and himself for the teleportation spell, but his father's magic felt much heavier than his own. It pulled Kyren from his worries and helped him focus on their mission, no matter how much he dreaded it.

They landed in the middle of the Magi camp. It took the sleeping Magi by surprise, but they were resourceful and immediately leapt into action.

One of the Magi men jumped up and slammed his hands onto the ground. An invisible force threw Kyren against the hardened ground and pinned him there. *Dark Blast!* Upon the command inside his mind, Kyren held out his hands, palms facing the sky, and shoved against the Magi's gravity.

The force of the explosion sent both Kyren and the Magi stumbling back a few feet. Kyren staggered to his feet, unbothered by the bruises and the blow that knocked his breath out. He'd had much, much worse from his father.

*Entrapment!* As Kyren formed his darkness into a cage to wrap around the Gravity Mage, the man used his energy to lift the entire cage into the air. Kyren cursed and cast a second spell, *Dark Sphere.* It wrapped around the Gravity Magi, cage and all, and slowly closed in against him.

"I want them alive," Vaxon snapped as he wrapped dark chains around two Magi brothers. For a moment, Kyren was distracted. The brothers had once been Kyren's close friends, Reth and Nyk.

He swallowed deeply but Vaxon shot him a glare. "I didn't bring you along to lose, weakling! I trust you remember what's at stake."

*Yes.* The pang of guilt and pain in his chest made it hard to breathe. His family. They would die if he didn't help his father capture the Magi, most of whom had once been his friends. He had to betray his old friends to ensure the safety of his family, even though doing so meant the death of all the captured Magi.

By then, the Gravity Mage had broken free of Kyren's sphere.

At this point, Kyren just wanted the fight to be over. *Bind!* Kyren thought the spell and it immediately took hold. Darkness wound around the Gravity Mage's legs, dragging him to the ground. Soon it bound his entire body there and he was unable to move or cast magic. It wouldn't last long, but it lasted long enough for Vaxon's guards to swoop in and bind the Gravity Mage with anti-magic chains.

He glanced at Vaxon as his guards arrested Reth and Nyk and took the three Magi away.

# JOANNA WHITE

With their defeat, the number of Magi Vaxon had captured totaled thirty-four.

# DARK MAGI

## CHAPTER THREE

WITH EACH OF his own people that were dragged into Vaxon's dungeons, each one beaten, each one torn away from their families, Kyren's chest filled with thousands of tiny needles.

He hated what Vaxon was doing. Despised it. But he could do nothing.

*No,* Kyren thought, *I am doing something. I'm helping him.*

The instant his mother entered the room, he concentrated on the room around him to empty out his thoughts. She had used telepathy to torment him his entire life.

Learning how to shut off his mind and emotions had been necessary to survive both his parents.

"Is it true this one did not even put up a fight?" She strolled into the room.

Kyren couldn't help but admire her grace and beauty. To distract himself from how normal she appeared, despite the beast that was her soul, he looked back down at the Magi on the table and shrugged. "Nope. This one is a Healer Wizard. He was caught trying to save a few of our men," Kyren explained.

Vassti scoffed.

The Healer Wizard mumbled under his breath. Kyren focused on the interrogation room to keep Vassti from finding out what it was. *Whatever spell you're casting, Healer, do it quickly,* he thought, keeping it tucked carefully away from his prying mother. "Well, he's finally awake," Kyren said.

Vassti gently pushed the Healer's hair out of his eyes. "Well, well... Eiridan Stormblessed. I'm not entirely sure why, but I thought you would be something.... more. All of the stories villagers told spoke of how brave and gallant you were. A hero. Nothing but lies, apparently, because you're a sniveling coward." At first, Vassti had sounded innocent and sweet—the tone of a loving mother, but the longer she spoke, the more malice and hatred seeped into her tone.

"I'm a coward?" the Healer murmured.

Though Vassti's words were sweet, her mouth curled into a snarl. "Yes, you are. Had you fought back, perhaps you would

# DARK MAGI

have given yourself a chance. Now, you're collared. Just like the dog you are."

Kyren clenched his hands into fists, struggling to control his anger. No matter what, he couldn't risk Ashyra being hurt because he had lashed out, either mentally or physically. *Say something,* he urged the Healer. More than anything, he just wanted to hear someone call his mother out; it would make his day.

Suddenly, his mother flinched.

Kyren looked at her in shock, and then confusion. He had never seen her wince or flinch before. He shifted his gaze back to the Healer, who hadn't moved. *What did he do to her?*

"Take him to the dungeons and throw him in with that spitfire, Jaeyria, and her companion. Perhaps they'll knock some sense into this idiot." With those words, Vassti rushed from the room.

"Your mother…she's… she's…" The healer only stared at Kyren with expressions of pity and concern.

Kyren smirked. "Demanding? Manipulative? Cruel?" *Hideous witch?* he silently added in his head.

"No," the healer stated. "Hurt. Her aura… It's cracked. Have you ever tried to ask her why?"

Kyren blinked. *Why in the world would I care about what she's feeling? I'm not exactly going to ask her any questions. Especially ones I don't want to know the answers to.* Sighing, he rubbed his eyes and crossed his arms. "I don't see people's auras. And no. She's not exactly the heart-to-heart kind of person," he said instead. *Every single day of my life that woman has pried into my mind, knowing every single thing about me. All my strengths, thoughts, weakness... She has always used everything against me. Everything,* Kyren thought bitterly with a sigh.

"I thought not. Well, since I'm clearly a prisoner, what's next?" the Healer asked.

"Why are you cooperating with us?" Kyren narrowed his eyes on the young man.

"Do I have a choice?"

"No," Kyren answered simply. *None of us do,* he added mentally.

"Then why fight? Besides, I don't want to hurt any of you."

Kyren only shook his head and laughed mirthlessly. "Sure you don't..." *The Magi have every right to hate the royal family. Most probably want to kill us. All of us. Not that I blame them.*

# DARK MAGI

"I really don't. The Father... He teaches us to love and have compassion on others."

Kyren had heard Ashyra say that many times, but growing up beneath Vaxon and Vassti's cruelty had taught him a completely different lesson. Did true compassion and kindness exist on this world? Did it exist anywhere, outside of the Father and His Son?

When Kyren stayed silent, the Healer continued speaking. "You're in more pain than she is, aren't you?" The Healer caught Kyren off guard. "She's learned how to handle it. How to block it out and feel nothing but what she wants to most of the time. But you haven't. You hide it behind your sarcasm and a brittle smile."

Staying quiet would only confirm the healer's words, but Kyren hated how true they were. *I may try to hide my thoughts from Vassti as much as I have learned to, but none of that stops the pain.* At the thought, Ashyra's face came to his mind, along with both of their children.

Just as soon as the images came to mind, he pushed them back. "You're a weird sort, Eiridan Stormblessed," Kyren murmured as he unlocked the Healer's chains.

"Maybe..."

Kyren sighed, feeling a pang of guilt in his chest. "A word of advice, Magi. Where you're going, kindheartedness will get you killed. I'm not going to be kind or forgiving when we meet for your final fight. And if you don't even try, you'll die for sure. No one else is going to back down once they find out what's at stake here."

"What is at stake?"

"Families. Happiness. Love." With each word, a new memory flashed in Kyren's mind. His and Ashyra's secret wedding, Kyren playing with his son in the servants' quarters, the moment he had first laid eyes on his little girl…

"What's he taken from you? You're sad about something…"

Kyren wanted to clench his jaw or punch something, but he no longer had the energy. He hated how perceptive the Healer was. "My wife and children." He hadn't meant to say the words, but somehow, they found their way out of his lips and into open air.

"Ah… I'm sorry, Kyren. Losing people, especially those you love, is the worst feeling possible. I wish I could heal you… The Father can. If you let Him."

Kyren frowned and didn't respond. What could he say to that? Could the Father really heal him? Would He, after what

# DARK MAGI

Kyren agreed to do for his father to protect his family? Kyren honestly didn't know.

"Kyren?" Eiridan blinked up at him.

"What?"

"Forgive him."

Those two worlds rattled Kyren's entire world. *"Forgive him?"* Kyren demanded harshly. "What are you anyway? A mind-reader like my mother?" His hands clenched in anger and hatred—immediate hatred for anyone just like his mother. *Get out of my head!*

Kyren grabbed the Healer and began dragging him down to the dungeon as the man explained that he could see auras because he was a healer. The last few words the Healer Wizard spoke Kyren completely ignored, forgetting they were ever stated in the first place.

"Save it for someone who cares," he snapped just before he shoved Eiridan out of the room and down the hallway.

As they walked, Eiridan asked him something odd. "Did… any of the Magi escape?" He choked, as if he couldn't breathe. It was the same tone Kyren had any time he asked about Ashyra.

"No. I'm sorry they didn't get away." Kyren didn't even bother fighting against the guilt that weighed heavily on his shoulders. "Most of them are relatively uninjured, if it's any consolation. Jaeyria Lightwood isn't so well, though... My father snapped her wrist." Anger flared in his chest as he unlocked a cell and threw Eiridan inside.

"I wish this could be different," Kyren whispered just before he left the dungeon behind.

As he got to the top of the stairs, his anger returned at the sight of his thirteen-year-old sister, Nassia, bounding down the dungeon steps as if it was a carnival.

"Take me to the dungeon!" she demanded. "I want to see all the handsome prisoners!"

Kyren rolled his eyes, but gestured for her to follow him. Guards flanked her on either side. On their way back down, he silently plotted out ten different ways he could kill her.

The only thing that kept him from doing it was Ashyra and his family. Hating her enough to want to kill her, kept her from being another piece in Vaxon's game against him.

They strolled passed the endless row of cells until they came to Eiridan's where he slept with his head resting on a young woman's lap.

"Hey! Wake up!" Nassia shouted, trying to wake him up.

# DARK MAGI

The other woman glared at Nassia with all the fury of a cyclops. "Shut up, Nassia. He's asleep, and he's tired."

"Who gave you permission to order me around?" Nassia crossed her arms and huffed. *Oh here we go,* Kyren thought as he rolled his eyes.

Their arguing finally awoke Eiridan, and Kyren wasn't surprised when the foolish Healer Wizard was nice to Nassia, only fueling the other woman's anger and jealously. It looked as if the woman was about ready to take off Nassia' head.

Kyren stepped forward from where he had leaned against the wall. Hating her was one thing; allowing her to get hurt or killed while she was in his care was another. With a mental curse, he readied himself in case the woman foolishly tried to attack his sister.

The woman only shoved her backwards into the grime on the floor.

Kyren wanted to laugh, but stayed quiet as Nassia ranted.

"Hey, Kyren?" the woman asked, looking at him.

He smirked at her. "You don't think I'm going to let you get away with hurting my sister, do you?" He sincerely hoped she figured out what he meant. *Please do more than dirty her pretty little dress.* Why did he

**33**

care? Why did he want the woman to do worse to Nassia? *Because she needs to learn to survive around father when I'm gone. Without me... What if he turns his attentions on her?* The thought terrified him more than he thought possible.

"Oh please. You can't possibly tell me that you don't wish she'd grow up and stop being such a nightmare." The woman scoffed.

"Regardless of what I wish, I'm not going to let you mistreat her." The lie slipped from his lips just as easily as breathing. Vaxon was watching, and even if he wasn't, Vassti wasn't too far away and she would mentally hear what happened.

He ignored the rest of the conversation. It mostly consisted of the woman Magi attempting to threaten Nassia, with Eiridan trying and failing to calm her down.

To distract Nassia so that she wouldn't choose to have someone executed, Kyren showed her the other Magi. She stopped in front of a cell across the hall. As she prattled on to the poor men she had chosen as her next interests, Kyren yawned and tried to keep from falling asleep.

"Are you really Daddy's other son?" she asked.

# DARK MAGI

Kyren's eyes snapped open as he looked at who she was talking about. Sure enough, it was Keldyr, the fire mage rumored to be Vaxon's illegitimate son.

Kyren clenched his jaw, and more than anything he just wanted to leave.

"Vaxon Asherex is not my father," Keldyr snapped.

Nassia frowned, then turned to flirt with the other Magi in the same cell.

"I've said this about practically every other male Magi, but this time I'm sure. You're the most handsome one of all. All quiet and mysterious and interesting."

While the two Magi in the cell snapped back at her, Kyren stepped closer to the bars and glanced at Keldyr. "You really are his other son, aren't you?"

Keldyr snarled at him. "Prince Kyren. Or should I say Slave Kyren? From the rumors it seems Daddy isn't too happy with you." His tone dripped with venom.

Kyren kept his face impassive, showing the man nothing of how his comments stung. "How did he find you?"

"I don't see how that's your business." Keldyr glared at him.

Kyren shrugged. "It's not like you would have been easy to find."

Keldyr leapt up and gripped the bars so tightly his knuckles turned white, even though his face was bright red with anger. "What? Trying to remind me that our father never cared about me and just left my mother and me? Do you—" He choked and rattled the bars of the cell with a furious curse. "Do you have any idea what my mother went through because of him?"

Kyren swallowed deeply and for once, let the pain show in his expression. "Yes. I do. I know what our scum of a father has done to me, to all the Magi, to everyone here."

Keldyr backed away as if he had been punched. He slowly slid down until he leaned against the wall in the corner.

"Might I remind you that you have a sister? It would be nothing for me to... I don't know; order one of the guards to cut her nose off." Nassia glared at the Magi with red eyes and white hair. Kyren nearly gasped. It was his old friend Reth.

Reth narrowed his eyes as his hands trembled against the cell wall. Reth's brother and another one of Kyren's old friends, Nyk, gripped Reth's arm. "Leave it alone," Nyk muttered to his brother, his silver eyes flashing. With a tense smile, he inclined his head to Nassia. "Princess, may I just apologize for my brother Reth's... hasty comments."

# DARK MAGI

Nassia stuck her chin up. "That's much better. I think I like you more than your brother. You won't be punished, but he still deserves it."

"Do whatever you want to me, you witch," Reth snapped. He spit toward her and even though it landed in the cell by the bars, Nassia leapt back. Kyren would have laughed; Reth had always been a bit... fiery, but he knew Nassia's temper and his old friends would pay if they weren't careful.

She cried out with fury and glared up at one of the guards with her. "Drag him out here and see to it that he's flogged. How dare you speak to me in such a manner?"

Kyren sighed. "Why did you have to ruffle my sister's feathers, Reth?"

Nyk stood in front of his brother, eyes pleading with Kyren. "Please... I will take my brother's due punishment. For the sake of what we once were..." In his eyes, Kyren could see the unspoken comment in them: *even though you're a traitor to us.*

Kyren glanced down at Nassia. Technically, as a slave and with Ashyra's life at risk, he had no say over what happened to them. He hated it, but there was nothing he could do.

Nassia waved him off. "No, no. I'm a good person and a merciful princess. I'll punish only your brother."

Reth shoved Nyk back, which was amusing considering Nyk was taller. "Let her do whatever she wants."

"Reth, don't." Nyk desperately pushed Reth behind him and glanced back at Nassia. "Please, my princess... I beg of you."

"Beg?" Nassia cocked her head with a devilish smile. "Perhaps if you were to beg of me properly... I might be persuaded to let this go."

"Nyk, don't lower yourself for her! Just go ahead and punish me!" Reth shouted, his shoulder length white hair contrasting his blazing red eyes.

"Nassia, my lovely!" Jahad strode down the hallway in between the rows of cells packed with Magi until he knelt down in front of Nassia.

"Uncle Jahad!" she beamed, embracing him.

"I do believe you are missing out on quite the delicacies upstairs. Why don't you head on up and I will meet you there? We can try some of that new Sea Sauce, alright?" Jahad smiled at her, ignoring the grime from the dungeon floor that soiled his pants.

Nassia bobbed her head up in down. "See you there!" With that, she trotted off and Kyren found it difficult to know how to feel about her. The annoying thirteen-year-old had made not only his life miserable but everyone around her. She enjoyed tormenting others almost more than Vaxon himself did. Perhaps that was where she inherited it from. She was still his sister but perhaps it was hard for him to admit that he cared precisely because she had so much Vaxon in her.

Jahad glanced at the two brothers in the cell. Neither had relaxed and each had a different fighting stance, ready to attack should the need arise. Kyren couldn't blame them. "I apologize for Nassia. Why don't you tell me your names?" Jahad stood up and pulled over a stool. He placed it in front of the bars of the cell and then looked up at the two Magi.

"Nyk," said the black-haired, silver-eyed one. "This is my brother, Reth."

Jahad reached to his belt where he had a canteen attached. "Would you like some water?"

"We don't want—" Reth started with a hate filled tone, but Nyk snatched his arm.

"Politely, we must decline," he murmured softly.

Jahad stood from the stool and held the canteen to the bars. "I promise you, it isn't poisoned."

Kyren kept his arms crossed and smirked at them. "My father has more creative ways of killing you both than poison. It's fine."

Slowly, Nyk nodded, grabbed the canteen, and slipped it through the bars. He handed it to his brother first, who drank from it. When he finished, he handed it to Nyk, who took a sip and slipped it back to Jahad.

He tied it back onto the belt around his waist and returned to his seat on the stool. "Now, would you two like to tell me your story? Where do you come from?"

Kyren shook his head and stalked off with a low growl. In a short time, he would have to fight and kill all of these Magi. He had no interest in getting to know them or in befriending them once again. It was hard enough to know he had betrayed them all, especially Reth and Nyk, two men who had once been his closest friends. Unfortunately, no matter how much he desperately wanted to leave the dungeon behind, he couldn't. Vaxon had ordered him to stay in the dungeon and help with keeping the Magi in control, so as soon as he stepped out the doors, he leaned against the wall and waited by the staircase that led back down inside.

It wasn't long before Jahad emerged from the dungeon steps. "You know the only reason why you go down there and ask them for their life stories is because you feel guilty over what happened." Kyren hadn't meant to snap at his uncle, but so much had happened in such a short time, and his worry for Ashyra and his children kept him in a horrible mood.

Jahad blinked back unshed tears, tears that Kyren knew Jahad would never shed until Vaxon was dead and had paid for what he did. He simply put a hand on Kyren's shoulder and walked away.

*Mathas.*

Kyren tried to ignore the pain that twisted his stomach into knots every time he thought of his old mentor and grandfather.

Before Jahad's hand turned the doorknob to the exit from the dungeon building, he stopped. "I do it because they were all Mathas' children. Not just Vaxon and me. Mathas not only trained them, but loved them, kept them safe in a world his own son destroyed and tore apart. I do it to honor his memory."

Kyren glared at the ground, thinking back to the day that Mathas had been executed. Kyren and Jahad both knew Mathas had only sacrificed himself so the other Magi students could escape Vaxon.

But neither of them had believed Vaxon had it inside him to kill his own father, to behead him like a common criminal, and then hang it from the city gates.

*"Father, please! Let him go!" Kyren fell to his knees, begging and pleading with him. The young seventeen-year-old boy should have known better than to believe Vaxon would ever do any such kind act.*

*Mathas willingly surrendered himself to Vaxon to distract him. It allowed all the other Magi students to escape. The moment Vaxon had brought Mathas into the dungeon where Kyren had been kept for the past day, Kyren had started to lose all hope.*

*Now, he had been chained to the front stand, giving him a perfect few of the block where Mathas knelt. Briefly his eyes met Kyren's. "All will be well," he murmured softly. No one in the crowd made a sound, so his murmur sounded louder.*

*Vaxon snarled at his father, clenching an axe formed out of darkness in his hands. "Even now at your end, you hold onto that bitter hope…"*

*"The Father's Light will embrace me soon, because of what the Son has done."*

*"Son?" Vaxon scoffed, pacing around behind the older Magi.*

*Kyren swallowed deeply.*

*"Your beliefs will die with you, old man. Just know that one day, I will corrupt*

# DARK MAGI

*my son that you stole from me!" Vaxon cried out in fury and brought the axe down upon Mathas' head.*

Kyren cursed, pushing the images from his mind. Without a reply to Jahad, he stormed out of the dungeon room.

Not for the first time, he felt as if his family was a curse.

# JOANNA WHITE

## CHAPTER FOUR

IT HAD ALWAYS been Ashyra to pray to the Father and the Son for their family. When neither of them knew how they would keep her pregnancy a secret, knowing that if Vaxon found out he would kill the child, it was she who had prayed for Ren to live and be protected from Vaxon's wrath—and he had. It was she who had prayed for little Rya. It was she who had prayed for Kyren's redemption.

Now, as he was escorted by six Nires guards, hands in anti-magic chains, Kyren's heart raced and he wondered if his prayers would even be heard. Today was the day that he and the other Magi would be thrown in the arena Vaxon had created, the day he would be expected to slaughter his own people and friends.

How could he?

# DARK MAGI

*Kyren held Ashyra's shoulders as they stood in a shed at the back of the palace grounds, where they had met so many times before. It was here that Ashyra had let him cry when he thought he was going crazy from trauma of his time in the dungeon, here where she had nursed his wounds any time he had been viciously flogged to the point of near death. As she bandaged him up, she sang songs of the Father, of His Light, and of His Son, so much so that Kyren needed to hear more.*

*"The Father's Light and Presence is always with us," Ashyra would tell him. They would pray together and Kyren's battered, broken body would sleep to her songs. For the first time in his life, he felt truly at peace.*

*The night he wanted to hang himself, it was Ashyra who had stopped him. She had shouted at him to tell him how important he was to her, then she had kissed him—their first kiss.*

*Now, as he held her shoulders, she refused to meet his gaze and she gnawed on her lower lip—a sign he knew meant something was truly* wrong.

*"Ashyra... What—are you tired of the secrecy? Are you leaving me?" It was the first question on Kyren's mind. Everyone hated him, everyone left him. He was never*

*good enough for anyone else. His father tortured and tormented him. Maybe he deserved to have Ashyra leave him.*

*Ashyra shook her head. "No! It isn't that..."*

*"Then what? Tell me..." Kyren desperately met her eyes and his hands automatically tightened on her shoulders of their own accord.*

*"I'm pregnant."*

*Those words had brought more life and light into him than he ever imagined or thought possible.*

With his family at stake…How could he choose between his friends and his family?

How could he not?

"I wanted to give you the proper motivation for killing those Magi scum," Vaxon said. He stood in front of the door to a special chamber far below the regular dungeon. Kyren couldn't stop the wince that shook his entire body. He had spent five years trapped and tortured here.

Kyren swallowed deeply.

Vaxon opened up the door and the Nires shoved him inside. Two stayed on either side of him while another one connected the end of the chains on his wrists to an iron ring on the wall behind him. They tightened it so that he had little maneuvering room. "Five minutes," Vaxon snapped.

The door slammed shut.

He stared at the sadistic and twisted devices, trembling. Tears burned in Kyren's eyes and he forgot everything else. He was back here and the pain all over his body was tangible.

"Kyren!" Just like it always had, Ashyra's beautiful, bubbly voice yanked him out of the attack. Kyren's gaze shifted to his wife. She darted up to him and embraced him with tears streaming down her face, black curls matted and tangled, but he didn't care.

He kissed her as passionately as he could, quick, hot, and desperate, like so many of their other kisses had been. A relationship in secret often meant their moments together had been rare and precious.

Ashyra leaned away and showed him their little girl Rya. She slept peacefully in her mother's left arm, oblivious to the world and all its troubles, unaware of the danger she was in. "I didn't think Vaxon would let you see us."

Kyren closed his eyes and breathed in her scent of roses, mixed with tears. "He wanted to remind me."

"Remind you?"

# JOANNA WHITE

Kyren shook his head, opening his eyes with a mirthless laugh. Tears fell from his eyes. Being around Ashyra again, even if he was in chains, felt like finally being able to breathe again after suffocating in smoke. "Are you and the kids unharmed?"

Ashyra nodded and then gestured to Ren.

His little two-year-old body toddled over to Kyren with a huge grin on his face. "Papa! You're here!"

"Yes, I'm here!" No matter the circumstances, his son always brought a smile to Kyren's face. The boy leapt up into his arms and Kyren tried to catch him, but the chains on his wrists prevented it. Just before Ren fell to the ground, Ashyra managed to catch him with her free hand. "Careful, Ren. I'm sorry. I can't hold you." Kyren knelt down and nuzzled his son's neck. "Remember your prayers and be good for your mother."

"I will. Always. Umm…Papa?"

"Yeah?" Kyren met his son's gaze.

Ren pointed to some of the devices in the room. "Mommy said those are bad. I—I don't want to be here. I'm scared."

"I know you're scared…" Kyren's heart hammered in his chest. He was absolutely terrified; for his family, for the Magi, for the terrible things he would have to do. "But it's okay to be scared. The Father will protect you. Just pray to Him and tell him what you're feeling. Okay?"

Ren bobbed his head up and down.

"What about your family? The alliance?" Kyren met Ashyra's calming eyes as Ren clung to his leg, wrapping his tiny little arms around his knee.

Ashyra shook her head. "I—I don't know. They're terrified of Vaxon. I've been hostage here for years and not once have they tried to rescue me. They haven't even sent me any word—no letters, nothing."

Kyren gnawed on his lip. He had hoped they would at least try, now that her life was in danger. What he didn't want to tell her was that Vaxon was cruel enough that he would kill her if Kyren disobeyed and forced his hand, despite the alliance that he needed. Now, the only way to ensure she and the children lived would be to obey him so Vaxon would let them live and send them home safely to Ashyra's family.

The door opened and six Nires guards strode into the room. Two of them shoved Ashyra and Rya back and slammed her up against the wall. Another guard gripped Ren's arms and yanked him off of Kyren's leg.

"Already? No! Kyren... Kyren, I see you! *I see you.*" Ashyra cried with a sob.

Their special phrase always brought warmth to Kyren's heart, but not now. Now it only brought him fear, fear that he would never see them again.

"I see *you!* I love you three, okay? Know that I will always love you!" Kyren shouted as the Nires unchained him and dragged him from the room. As they closed and locked the door behind him, the ones holding him threw him at Vaxon's feet.

"Do you know why I brought them here?" Vaxon's voice was deep and full of hatred and darkness, as it always had been.

Kyren closed his eyes, willing the tears away but they stayed with him as he nodded. "Yes," he whispered. The weight of what Vaxon was doing sat so heavily upon him he could hardly breathe. The only reason Vaxon had brought him here was to be assured that Kyren would fall into line and obey him. "If—if I don't obey you…"

Vaxon smirked down at him, speaking casually as if the conversation were about dinner. "I'm using plenty of magical spells and devices to watch everything that goes on in that arena. If you fail to kill anyone, if you let any of them go… The moment that you hesitate or show any weakness, I'll come straight here and begin my work. You know how skillful I am at such things… An expert really." Vaxon shrugged. "I will kill your family, starting with your wife. How long do you think she would last in here? Not as long as you, Kyren."

Kyren closed his eyes and couldn't help the tears that fell. Images appeared in his mind, some memories, some his worst fears. Vaxon torturing Ashyra... He collapsed on all fours with a quiet, hoarse sob. "I'll kill whoever you want. J—just please let them live." Before his father, he was helpless. Even if he killed whomever his father wanted, Vaxon could still kill his family out of spite. "Let them live," he begged, barely above a whisper.

Vaxon growled.

Kyren opened his eyes and met Vaxon's gaze. "What do you want from me? Other than to kill Magi and to die in the arena with them?" Fear coursed through his veins but it mixed with a fierce determination to save his family...

No matter the cost.

Vaxon grinned. "What do I want? For you to die, Kyren. You rebelled against me, sided with your grandfather and the Magi against me, chose their beliefs over mine. I will never forgive you."

*Torturing me for five years wasn't enough?* But the words caught in Kyren's throat.

# JOANNA WHITE

"Ever since then, *you have been no son of mine.*"

*I chose the Father and His Son,* Kyren wanted to say, but he stayed quiet, unwilling to risk his father's wrath. He had no idea how Vaxon could speak so casually about killing his own father, then again... The terrible things he was comfortable doing to a mother and her children were unspeakable, so it shouldn't have been surprising. Kyren often wondered what had happened to make his father this way. He tried to imagine a younger Vaxon who wasn't evil, but it was impossible.

"But I might be willing to give you a second chance. If you somehow managed to kill *all* the Magi and still stay alive against whatever I send your way..." Vaxon shrugged. "You could become the son I want you to. Embrace the darkness. Choose me over the beliefs that your grandfather foolishly instilled in you. Kill and kill well to dishonor your grandfather and his teachings inside you. I'll banish Ashyra and your children back to her kingdom, but they'll live. And you will obey me, never to rebel again."

Kyren hung his head. No matter what he did, he would never see his family again. But at least, if he obeyed his father... embraced evil and did what Vaxon wanted,

# DARK MAGI

Ashyra, Ren, and Rya would live. They wouldn't be viciously and brutally tortured. No, they would live long, free, happy lives somewhere in the world, away from all of this, maybe even off planet and away from Castre.

"I'll do it."

# CHAPTER FIVE

KYREN HATED THE waiting more than anything. He just wanted to be let loose, away from the chains and anti-magic walls that confined him and the other thirty-four Magi inside the bottom of a stone tower. At this point, Kyren had accepted his fate, so he just wanted to kill them and end his life to be done with it all.

The sooner it began, the sooner it would end.

A wild Gravity Mage named Jesyth snapped at him several times, but Kyren allowed it to roll off of him like waves. "You tore us from our families!" Jesyth shouted at him. "Now they're in danger just as much as we are!"

Kyren's mind instantly conjured up images of Ashyra, his son Ren, and his little girl—Rya.

Once, Kyren had almost lost Ashyra.

# DARK MAGI

Kyren paced nervously outside a shed at the back of the palace grounds—their special place—palms sweaty and clammy.

Another slave was in there with her while Ashyra gave birth to Ren. Since they had lied, Vaxon believed it was a guard's illegitimate child, so he gave Ashyra no care. Her screams lasted for hours and each one made Kyren wince.

What would he do without her? Her love and light and life made him who he was. She had led him to the Father; she loved him when no one else had. She had saved his life when he only wanted to die. It was Ashyra who had brought him back from the darkness that he had been forced to embrace to survive all those years being tortured. She brought him back from madness and showed him a love and light and compassion and kindness that Kyren had never even believed existed in the world.

Without her, his mind returned to the pain, to the darkness he feared.

Jahad, his uncle, placed a comforting hand on Kyren's shoulder. "Trust in the Father and His Son."

Kyren was too nervous to do anything in that moment except pace.

Suddenly, the slave darted out the shed door, staring at him with tears in her *eyes. "Kyren, you have a boy, but... she's bleeding too much and I can't stop it."*

*"No!" Kyren cried as he darted into the room. His son lay on the floor wrapped in cloth, still bloody. Ashyra lay on the floor of the shed, breathing shallowly. Her eyes were closed and he gripped her hand. Tears fell from his eyes, dripping onto her face. "Father, I have not been a good man, or followed you until I met Ashyra. I—I can't lose her. You—you know what awaits me if she dies. I don't—I don't want to go back to living a loveless life filled with darkness and torture. Please—" Kyren choked, collapsing onto the floor beside his precious, beautiful wife. "Please save her..."*

*Minutes later, the bleeding stopped and she awoke. Kyren held his son for the first time as he and Ashyra laughed and smiled at Ren's adorable, chubby cheeks.*

*Now Kyren had two lights in his life, not just one.*

"Ren," he whispered. "Ashyra…Rya. "Father, I have not been a good man. You— you know what waits for me without her, without our children. Please, don't make me go back to living a loveless life filled with darkness and pain. Please—" Kyren choked and closed his eyes, breathing deeply to try to reign in his emotions.

# DARK MAGI

He wasn't sure how long they were forced to wait, but the longer they did, the more memories came to his mind. Thinking of Ashyra, Ren, and Rya only brought him more pain. They were captured and would be killed if he didn't betray the Magi, and murder innocent people, most of whom had once been his friends.

In that moment, his heart broke, but Ashyra... his children.... were the first good thing that had come into his life. They were lights in his world of pain, suffering, and darkness.

To distract himself, he thought of Jahad and all the warnings he had given.

*"The... arena Vaxon has created will have supplies scattered throughout it, but Kyren, be careful. Each cache is guarded by dangerous and ancient creatures."*

*Kyren frowned. "Why give us supplies if we are all meant to die in there?"*

*Jahad hung his head sorrowfully. "You know how sadistic your father is, Nephew. He wants to prolong it. Some Magi are meant to die while others are meant to be sparred and tormented later. If the Magi fought over resources, it would be entertaining and he wants to see them turn on each other. He wants to see them turn into the evil they tried to destroy. When the people see this, it will ensure no one else dares rebel against him like the Magi tried to do."*

*Kyren swallowed deeply.*

*"One more thing," Jahad said, placing his hand on his nephew's shoulder. "There will be several caves, each with magical artifacts inside them. After day or two, you need to find a cave and grab one of the magical objects. They're highly important."*

*"What are they for?" Kyren asked.*

*Jahad shook his head. "To cure you of anti-magic gas. Only the strong will survive, which will make it more entertaining. Each Magi has a specific cave. Make sure you find one and survive."*

*Kyren had no idea why his uncle was trying so hard to keep him alive. Escape would be impossible and his death was assured. Vaxon had carefully and meticulously planned every detail of this out, especially ensuring no one could escape the arena. But he couldn't bring himself to remind Jahad of his fate.*

*"The Father's Light guide you," Jahad murmured to him softly.*

*With the dark acts Kyren would have to commit to keep his family alive, Kyren doubted the Father's Light would reach him at all.*

# DARK MAGI

Suddenly, the chains released and the gate opposite from Kyren was lifted. As soon as it completely disappeared, the thirty-four Magi poured out.

The cracked walls were soon replaced with the open air of the valley as he sprinted out of the tower. Kyren gazed around in wonder. Tall trees rose to the sky, layered upon the hills on either side of the valley. A river snaked through the center, dividing the valley in two. Howls and hisses of the creatures within the forest echoed throughout the entire area. Several of the Magi scattered into the trees of the forest. Moments later, Kyren could hear the sounds of some of the Magi screaming. Far in the distance, surrounding the whole valley, the anti-magic dome shimmered brightly.

"Well, shall we fight then?" Kyren asked. His automatic response was to hide his pain with sarcasm. A few Magi that had families under threat from Vaxon stayed to fight each other as the rest finished fleeing.

One caught his eye: Reth, his old friend with his back turned.

Kyren grinned. As his old friend turned around, Kyren called darkness to his fist and punched Reth. Reth reeled back from the blow, but charged toward him.

Kyren teleported behind him. *Dark cloud.* It shot out and knocked Reth down.

# JOANNA WHITE

The hairs on Kyren's neck stood up, diverting his attention as he sensed shadow magic. *Cloak.* He pulled darkness over him like a warm blanket.

Dryst, the other Shadow Sage, and his brother Daek, were fighting with a wolf and an earth mage, Vyu. Dryst threw the shadows forward like shards, coating the earth mage, who soon fell to the ground, dead.

Kyren still had plenty of energy, as he called the darkness forward in the shape of a spear and hurled it at Daek, just as Dryst's shadows wrapped around the wolf, suffocating it.

Daek blocked Kyren's spear, as the dead wolf turned into Mylo.

Kyren closed his eyes and shot dark lightning out of his hands. His energy and power coursed through his veins again. After ten years of not being able to use it, as the darkness tugged and pulled at him, he accepted it with open arms. All those years of denial had only built up his energy levels.

He could continue like this for hours.

Dryst summoned a shadow sword, so Kyren did the same with darkness. They danced around each other, clashing swords and dancing shadows.

Kyren formed darkness into a flaming ball, and threw it at Dryst, who

# DARK MAGI

caught it, forming it into shadows that snaked around Kyren's feet. Kyren drained them into his body, using them for more energy.

*Dark wave,* Kyren thought. As Dryst was distracted by the wave, Kyren formed a dark spear, and threw it at Daek. Daek was busy fending off another Magi and didn't see it coming.

It pierced his chest, and he fell to the ground with a gurgle.

Dryst charged toward Kyren with a wild cry. No part of him could deny that he enjoyed fighting and using his darkness to his full potential only fueled the wickedness inside him. "It's a shame how weak your brother was," Kyren taunted. "He won't be around to protect you anymore."

Dryst attacked him in blind rage, exactly as Kyren wanted. Once again, the two clashed swords. Kyren finally found an opening and stabbed him. Dryst collapsed to the ground, dying beside Daek's body.

"Who's next?" Kyren asked the other Magi around him. As Dryst died, Kyren drained the shadows away from him and used it to fuel his own energy.

Nyli started toward him, but before she could move, he threw darkness at her. It snaked around her arms, draining her energy. He pulled it to him, replacing what it took to cast the spell. *Dark drain,* he thought, holding it in his mind to keep up the spell.

It wasn't long before she lay dead on the ground.

As Shara used light to escape him, Kyren raised his hands, and thought, *blackout.* In an instant, his darkness dispelled all light within the area. It looked as if it was midnight despite the fact that it was still early morning.

Blue flames grew around him, pushing some of his darkness back. Before Kyren could pinpoint the source, it disappeared. He finally turned, forming darkness into an axe, ready to kill whoever was behind him.

With a curse, he realized it was a young girl. She was with the conjurer boy, both of them only fourteen years old. They looked at him in fear and scrambled backward.

Kyren knelt down beside them and wrapped darkness around them all. "I won't hurt you. I want to help you." He hated himself for doing this but he couldn't bring himself to kill two kids. Hopefully, his darkness was enough to hide that from Vaxon.

"Why should we trust you?" Erai demanded.

# DARK MAGI

"Because you're still alive." Kyren frowned when he thought about how easily he could kill them both. *Two seconds is all I would need to finish you both off.* Fortunately, his words convinced them to flee in the safety of the trees.

As he stood up, ensuring that they safely darted away, Nyk dashed toward him. Kyren called tendrils of darkness toward him. He expelled them out, blocking off Nyk's line of attack.

Nyk moved around him, using plants to slice away Kyren's darkness. Kyren twisted left and ducked down, barely avoiding him. He threw darkness toward Nyk in a wave. Nyk rolled underneath it and charged toward him with a plant dagger. Wrapping darkness around himself, Kyren teleported behind him.

To his surprise, Nyk just collapsed. Kyren laughed. "Have you already used up your energy? I thought you were smarter than that, old friend."

Light burst around Kyren, dispelling his darkness. He had no time to see where Nyk went, as he stood face to face with Yuknao. His energy levels were dwindling, so he would have to wait to finish Yuknao off later. "You're spared this time, Light Mage." With that, Kyren covered himself in darkness and teleported away.

He stood by a tree, panting. Sweat coated his face and his hands shook. *Oops. I've already pushed myself too far,* he thought. Kyren kept his eyes alert, watching every rock and tree around him to ensure he was alone. *I need to get to the Heart Tree...*

If only he would be allowed a break, but not now. The Magi had rebelled against Vaxon when he had stolen the throne, so now he wanted to magically broadcast their deaths with spells and magic devices. Knowing his father, Vaxon would expect Kyren to take part in the most deaths in the initial fighting. With Vaxon watching... Kyren could take no chances. For fear of Ashyra and his children's lives, Kyren only allowed himself a break when absolutely necessary. All Kyren wanted to do was teleport away from here, rescue his wife and children, and leave, but he couldn't. It was impossible.

None of them could escape, not with the anti-magic dome around the entire valley.

Tears burned in his eyes but he shoved them away. An evil man like him didn't deserve to cry for what he had done. Guilt washed over him, replacing the adrenaline and the instinct to fight and kill, to obey his father and try to keep his wife alive.

# DARK MAGI

What made him better than Vaxon?

Kyren knew the answer to that:

Nothing.

When he had fully recovered his energy, he drew darkness to him, disappearing into a cloud of smoke. He didn't really think of any place in particular, just appeared in an area at random, prepared to fight for supplies.

First he encountered the woman fire mage. She was already low on energy, and no match for him, at least until her brother showed up. He put up more of a fight, one that Kyren enjoyed. When Cathri lit the forest around him on fire and disappeared with her brother, Kyren cursed.

*Seriously? How many of them have just fled? Dryst and his brother were the only ones who put up a good fight, and now they're both dead.*

Suddenly, he collided with someone and fell on top of the female air mage.

Craving a fight, he pinned her legs and arms to held her down. Her wind did nothing against him, but she stopped and relaxed underneath him. *Come on. You're not putting up a fight, either?* Kyren cursed.

"Kill me. Get it over—behind you!"

In a rush, he jumped off of her and charged toward a Magi named Hammor who attacked him with a sword. He reacted too late, and Hammor would have killed him, if not for the gust of air that slammed against the other Magi. Hammor's body sprawled onto the ground, blood spurting from the wound on his head. Without even walking toward him, Kyren knew he was dead.

Kyren turned toward the Air Mage in shock. "He could've killed me." He wanted to ask her why she had not fought him, and yet had killed a fellow Magi for him. *Already they're turning against each other. Exactly what Vaxon wants.* Kyren's chest tightened bitterly. "Why would you do such an idiotic thing?"

"Do you have a family?" The question took him by surprise.

As Ashyra and his children's faces appeared in his mind, Kyren froze and realization struck him.

"That's why."

*Vaxon will never let me live. I'm going to die in here, so saving me and killing him was a waste. You killed a friend for nothing,* Kyren thought. He stood up and teleported away from her, figuring Vaxon would forgive him for letting her go since she had been way too easy. At least, he hoped Vaxon would forgive him. "I'll kill her later," Kyren muttered out loud, hoping and praying that would help.

# DARK MAGI

There had already been enough death.

# CHAPTER SIX

HIS TIME IN the arena had already proved an interesting one. Between his encounters with all the Magi and then a few run-ins with a pack of direwolves, Kyren finally had the chance to stretch his magic muscles. The entire arena, as Vaxon called it, was really just a wide valley surrounded by the anti-magic dome. In the weeks before the Magi had been dumped into it, Vaxon had unleashed creatures such as direwolves, phoenixes, griffins, and more into the valley and then found a way to keep them sectioned off in their own territories. The only place for Kyren to have a break was at the Heart Tree with the Elves since this was their land to begin with. Unfortunately, he didn't have the energy for a teleportation spell, so he trekked through the valley, staying close to the river until he arrived at the Heart Tree.

# DARK MAGI

It towered in the center of the Elf territory, and Kyren suspected its roots were sprouting up through the ground to create the trees in this part of the forest. They looked different than the normal oaks of the rest of the valley.

His breathing came in pants, and sweat once again coated his face. His hands shook and he struggled to keep his body from shivering. *Pushed myself too far.*

He could almost hear his grandfather scolding him. *"A wise Magi knows when to fight and when to flee. If you push yourself too far, you will end up killing yourself."*

*Shut it, Mathas. You're dead anyway.*

The Elves emerged from inside the Heart Tree, each one standing taller than a typical human man.

"Why have you come, Mage of Darkness?" the leader asked with a harsh accent.

Kyren shrugged. "Would you be willing to let me stay, eat, and rest?" He lifted an eyebrow.

"To earn the right to stay with us, you must face hand-to-hand combat with our mightiest warrior."

Kyren sighed. "Let's get this over with."

An Elf even taller than the leader leapt off the ground so high he landed a kick to Kyren's head while still in the air. Seeing stars and feeling pain crack through his skull, Kyren fell onto the ground but rolled to his feet and slammed his fist into the Elf's chest. He swung toward the Elf again, who expertly twisted out of the way.

Kyren stepped back, breathing heavily. Doing this while he was low on energy was not easy on him. The Elf lunged toward him and Kyren knocked the Elf's blow aside. From there, he struck the Elf's neck with an open palm and kneed him in the ribs. As the Elf doubled over, Kyren grabbed his head and slammed it against his knee.

The Elf fell, but yanked Kyren down with him. The Elf landed on top of him, hands around his throat.

"The fight is concluded." The voice came from the leader.

Coughing, Kyren stumbled to his knees. "Suppose you want me to leave now. Right?"

The leader shook his head. "You are a worthy opponent and thus, may stay."

The Elves fed Kyren the fruit from the Heart Tree and he chatted quietly with a few of the more talkative Elves while he rested to try to regain his magical energy. So

# DARK MAGI

far, it wasn't working. The worst part of it was that Vaxon ensured the anti-magic dome blocked Mathanos from coming in through the air. Essentially, the only Mathanos —magical energy that gave all Magi their power—they had to use was what little was in the air inside the arena. The more Magi who died meant less Magi to use up all the Mathanos in the air. Unfortunately, to kill them meant using more Mathanos. Without being able to draw in more energy, Kyren's reserves would take a long time to refill.

After about an hour, a young Magi woman walked into the group of Elves.

"Eriswen, the Shield Wizard, right?" Kyren stood and smirked at her. "What are you doing here?"

"I could ask the same of you. I know you've already killed several Magi. That's sick… turning on your own people like that."

Kyren shrugged. He didn't have to explain himself to her.

The leader stepped forward. "If you two wish to settle things, you will do it in the Way of Old."

"Without magic." Eriswen narrowed her eyes at Kyren but nodded to the leader's words.

Kyren grinned. That was fine with him.

"Begin."

At the leader's command, Kyren and Eriswen charged toward each other. Her leg whooshed toward his head, so he twisted to the right just in time to avoid it. Kyren slid in closer to her and elbowed her in the face but as she reeled back, she kicked his ribs, which he hadn't been expecting.

The two stepped back for a moment and stared at each other. He watched the way she moved her feet gracefully over the ground, barely taking a step. Then he finally spotted her pointed ears and realized why she had been accepted into the Elvish community without fighting a warrior first.

She was a half-Elf.

Kyren used a tree behind him to leap off of and he came down toward Eriswen's face with his foot. She used both her hands to block his foot and then front-kicked toward his chest. He caught her leg and flipped her onto the ground on her back.

She gasped for breath, but nailed him in his privates. He doubled over as pain rolled through him. That gave her enough time to climb on top of him and shove him onto his stomach. With a grunt, she grabbed his right arm and pinned it behind him.

# DARK MAGI

He growled and pressed all his weight onto his left arm as he rose to his hands and knees. She slipped her hands around his throat, or tried to, but as he balanced on his knees, he snatched her left hand with his. He wrenched it forward and pinned it at his side. "Now what?" he asked with a smirk.

She leaned down and bit his ear.

Fiery pain stabbed him where her teeth clamped down and he grabbed his ear with both his hands as she leapt off him. Before he had a chance to react, she kicked him in the face. The dizziness from his depleted magic energy worsened and the world around him spun so hard he had no idea where he was.

Just as she brought a dagger down toward him, Kyren teleported away. That drained his Mathanos even more, but he ignored it and sat down to rest on a rock near the sea, tired and irritable.

He could not imagine how long it must have taken Vaxon to place the anti-magic dome around such a gigantic area. The Valley Sea was massive in size but along the distant horizon, Kyren could see the anti-magic dome blocking off escape from that way too.

*Between using too much earlier, then all the running around and fighting, it's a wonder I haven't passed out yet,* Kyren's eyes slowly started to droop.

Far to the left, resting against the cliffs was Mermaid Cove with a cave cut inside the cliffs. He stumbled inside the damp cave, ignoring the waves lashing against the sharp rocks beneath his feet. His eyes snapped to the blonde Shadow Sage, Jaeyria, standing inside as she hurled shadows toward two figures in the back of the cave. *I've already killed one shadow mage today. Why not two?* he thought.

"What are you doing here?" she asked.

"Same as you, I'd say. I came for the supplies rumored to be here."

Kyren looked around, and noticed Eiridan kissing one of the sirens deeply. With a chuckle, Kyren shook his head. "He got himself into a pretty pickle."

"Why don't you just leave? I'm not exactly in the mood to fight you right now." Jaeyria glared at him ruthlessly.

Kyren smirked. "What? You upset that your boyfriend's kissing a siren? I'm guessing you don't have the Mathanos to separate them, do you? Either that or she's keeping you away from them somehow." He shrugged and called darkness to his hands.

The headache pounding his skull and dizziness causing the entire cave to tilt should have stopped him, but he formed the darkness in his hands into tendrils and hurled them toward her. It was the easiest attack, and one that didn't use up much of his energy.

He could almost hear Mathas lecturing him again. *I'm going to die here, might as well die from my own foolishness rather than letting one of the Magi kill me.*

Her shadow magic foolishly tried to tear away his darkness, but he laughed at her, leaning against the wall casually. Or at least, he hoped he appeared casual. The last thing he wanted was for Jae to realize he was weakening himself and on the verge of collapsing from the spinning world around him. Ignoring his own state of mind, Kyren swirled his tendrils around her, enjoying himself immensely by how furious he made her.

Before she could even write her runes in the air, he threw darkness at her again. The tendrils yanked her wrist, pulling her forward. As she landed at his feet, he sent the tendrils following after her, like pet snakes.

He looked at Eiridan. "He's going to be dead pretty soon if you don't find a way to save him." Kyren kept his back against the wall, pinning her with his dark tendrils.

A rune flashed on the floor beside Jaeyria on Kyren's left and shadows exploded around her. The shadows threw his tendrils against the Siren, who snapped her head up at him and hissed.

"Not good," Kyren muttered.

She released her hold on Eiridan and lunged straight for Kyren. If she touched him or if he heard her Siren's song…

No. He had to deal with this quickly.

With a groan, Kyren threw his hands forward, palms facing the siren and beams of darkness shot away from his palms and pierced her skull. She collapsed onto the ground, dead before she could spell him.

Jaeyria and Eiridan embraced. "Eiri, are you alright? Tell me you're alright!"

Eiridan nodded with a wheeze. "Y— yes. Just low on energy that's all. She nearly drained me."

Kyren gritted his teeth. *I'll never get to embrace Ashyra again.* He swallowed, desperately trying not to think about how he would never hold his children again either.

Jaeyria scrawled more runes onto the rocky surface beneath them.

Kyren snarled, forming a sword out of darkness, and held it to her throat. Images came to his mind, of Vaxon and his sorcerers surrounding Kyren's prison cell, drawing dark glyphs into the air, glyphs that brought agony and pain. He still felt the remnant pain inside his body. "What are you doing now?" Kyren pressed the sword tightly against her neck, struggling to push the images of Vaxon torturing him in the back of his conscious.

"I'm portaling us out of here, thank you very much!" Almost before the last word finished, she and Eiridan disappeared.

Kyren sat inside the cave as his mind drifted to thoughts of his wife and children, of them laughing and playing together. He had no idea that he had fallen asleep.

Sometime later, he woke, soaking wet, still inside Mermaid Cove. Waves crashed against the rocks and his back and skin ached—rocks didn't make the best beds. Stretching out his sore muscles, he searched the cave, but found no supplies. Either another Magi had already taken it, or Vaxon had lied and there was none. He used darkness to portal himself out, surprised another Siren hadn't found him while he was unconscious.

Some of his energy had returned but his head still pounded furiously against his skull, and exhaustion swept over him.

When he came to the griffin cliffs, he crouched down to avoid disturbing the majestic creatures. He desperately needed the supplies left there and he hated Vaxon

# JOANNA WHITE

for his extra cruelty. *He wants the Magi to all live as long as possible and die as slowly as possible. Not from starvation or lack of Mathanos. He wants them all to die in battle,* Kyren thought.

Just as he reached the cliff, he stopped, seeing a female Magi named Ashni.

"We got here at the same time. Who gets the pack? I suggest a duel, using magic only. Winner gets the supplies and leaves unharmed. Loser leaves with their life. If they're lucky. Deal?" *Kyren, you are an idiot. Challenging her to a duel with magic, when you don't have that much energy left to use? Are you trying to get yourself killed?* For some reason this time, it was Ashyra's voice yelling at him in his mind, not Mathas'.

*I'm a dead man walking. Might as well enjoy myself.* Kyren easily dodged a lightning strike she fired at him. As she called another one, he jumped away from it faster than he had the last. When she threw lightning at him in a ball of swirling energy, he cast a tendril toward it and then thought, *darkness disperse!* His tendril snuffed out the lightning, sending sparks flying everywhere. With that spell, he could feel energy leaving his body, and exhaled sharply, struggling to stay upright.

# DARK MAGI

*"The moment that you hesitate or show any weakness, I'll come straight here and begin my work. You know how skillful I am at such things..."* This Magi was strong and Vaxon would never forgive him if he let her go. And Vaxon would have already seen their fight, so hiding her and saving her life was out of the question.

No, he had to kill her. Or Vaxon would...

The things Vaxon would do to Ashyra before he killed her twisted Kyren's stomach and made him want to sob. He—he had no choice but to kill Ashni, regardless of how much he wanted to let her live.

*I'm sorry. Darkness drain,* he thought, throwing out darkness in the air. Kyren had already used the spell once already, but it was the quickest way to refill his own energy levels. His darkness swarmed around her, latching onto her body, dragging her energy away from her and into himself. Bile formed in the back of his throat at the newfound strength surging through his veins. *Her strength. Her energy.*

The feeling made him sick.

Remorse slithered through his veins. He cursed and tried desperately to shove it away, to avoid any weakness, but he couldn't. No one knew or understood what it felt like to have their energy taken away, to feel the darkness crawling inside them with no way to get it out, except Kyren. How many times had Vaxon cast this exact same spell on him?

With the darkness inside him, giving him strength and power, Kyren's desire to fight fled. He wanted to give up, wanted this to be over, prayed for something or someone to kill him so that his family could be safe and this could all be over. Every moment the spell drained Ashni brought a new image, a new memory of Vaxon casting the same spell on him. How many times had he collapsed onto his bed at night, exhausted and weakened, near the brink of death because Vaxon had taken his energy from him?

A griffin, as beautiful and majestic as the legends told, stood in between Kyren and the Lightning Mage. Kyren's darkness stopped and he stepped back, in shock. Grinding his teeth against one another, he glared at it. The spell fueled his darkness as well as his power, and for a brief moment, he *reveled* in feeling powerful once again.

Not a beaten and weakened slave.

Here, *he* had the power.

*This would be a good way to die.* At least he wouldn't die a weakling, underneath his father's cruel hand. No, in here, he would die what he always wanted to be: a warrior.

*No,* Mathas' voice whispered in his mind. *You will die a murderer. You will die known as someone who is just as cruel as your father. And that is not what you wanted. You just wanted to live with your wife and children, happy and together.*

"That's never going to happen!" Kyren screamed to the sky in pain and fury and sorrow. The griffin took off, along with the girl.

No longer having the desire to fight, Kyren walked aimlessly. It wasn't until he saw the female Gravity Mage, choking and killing Faeva, the woman who had loved his grandfather and mentor Mathas, that he stopped and snapped to his senses. After the loss of Kyren's grandmother, it had taken years before Mathas had finally found love again and Faeva had given it to him, the same way Ashyra had done for him.

Faeva.

Kyren stared at her in shock, watching as the Gravity Mage held her down and tried to kill her. Even though they were in an arena meant to fight each other to the death—and most of them had already turned on each other—it was still jarring to see them turn on one of the more helpless of the group of Magi. Even if there was some sort of false promise that their families would live if they did as Vaxon wanted. In that moment, Kyren knew that the Father would be ashamed of their actions this terrible day; his most of all.

*Faeva is pregnant with Mathas' child. My uncle. Vaxon's younger brother.*

Without thinking, Kyren charged toward her, creating an arrow out of darkness. It embedded into the Gravity Mage's throat, killing her.

Faeva sat up and stared at him in horror and shock.

He placed a finger over his mouth, and then called darkness to him, slinking into the shadows of the trees. When he emerged, he hoped it was a far enough distance away from her.

Suddenly, Vaxon appeared in front of him, coated in a blue hue. Ashyra was behind him, being held by two Nires as a palace guard began whipping her.

Kyren screamed at him, and darted forward, throwing darkness at the image in vain. "Leave her alone!"

Vaxon growled at him. "You not only saved the woman who is pregnant with my younger brother, but two children. You lost to the Shield Wizard who has tried to kill me. Worse, you spared the female Shadow Sage, along with the male Light

# DARK MAGI

Mage. You've spared too many. Now your wife is paying the price." He nodded his head and the Nires stopped.

Vaxon grabbed a vicious tool in his hand as the Nires shoved Ashyra onto the ground. In the background of the magical projection, Ren held little Rya, sobbing and begging the guards to leave them alone.

Kyren's heart sank.

Vaxon knelt beside Ashyra where she had been strapped down to the bed of spikes. He reached the tool down and carved through a piece of her skin on the back of her shoulder. Kyren knew without a doubt that Vaxon wouldn't stop until he flayed every inch of her body in front of him.

*I can't lose her,* he thought in horror. "I'll make it up to you!" Kyren shouted.

Vaxon held up a hand and whirled around to face him in fury. "Get rid of my illegitimate child, Keldyr, will you? Consider that your punishment."

Kyren clenched his jaw.

"But you must fulfil your mission…" Vaxon started with a sly grin, "My father's bloodline must die with Faeva. That brother of mine that lives inside her womb must die. Do you understand, Kyren?" Without waiting for a response, the image flickered and disappeared.

# JOANNA WHITE

Night had fallen, and stars twinkled overhead. It was as if they didn't notice the crimson blood staining the ground below it, as if they didn't realize how many Magi had died.

Keldyr was asleep nearby, camping out with a few other Magi. One of them stayed on lookout, so Kyren called darkness around him like a cloak, making him invisible. He used darkness to form a dagger in his hands. "I'm sorry..." Kyren choked.

With tears in his eyes, he stabbed the dagger into his half-brother's throat.

# DARK MAGI

## CHAPTER SEVEN

MORE THAN ANYTHING, Kyren just wanted to be left alone. Only one day and already the blood of Magi stained his hands… Even the blood of his half-brother.

And there was nothing he could do to stop it.

Then, there was the horrifying thought of how easily the Magi had turned on each other to keep their own families and friends alive. One of them, Nyk, had even agreed to work for Vaxon. Vaxon had appeared to Kyren, telling Kyren to spare Nyk due to their secret deal. How could his old friend have betrayed everyone for nothing? *You have done the same,* a voice in Kyren's mind whispered, but he argued with it. Everything he did—every deplorable, horrid act—was to save his wife and children. Nyk or his loved ones weren't under threat. He betrayed them because he chose to.

"Why did you save me?"

At the sound of a voice, Kyren was yanked from his thoughts, instantly forming a dagger out of darkness. His magic had finally regenerated, but his body was still exhausted from pushing himself so much the previous day. It was no surprise that his reactions were slower, that his body ached deeply, and he could hardly catch his breath. Using up too much magic came with a price.

The voice had come from Faeva. His grandfather's... new wife. His own uncle resided inside her stomach. Why had he saved her? Moral obligation? Perhaps, Kyren suspected, that had something to do with it. *It was because of Mathas. He trained me. Saved the Magi. Did everything in his power to keep Jahad and me safe from Vaxon. I owe him everything.*

"You're not here to help us, right? So why did you save me?"

A deep pain flared inside him. He had spared her once, Vaxon had seen, Ashyra had been tortured, and Kyren's punishment had been...

Killing his own brother.

"I know your secret," Kyren said, interrupting whatever she had been saying. "The entire court does, in fact. We know

# DARK MAGI

you carry his child. One of my tasks here is to make sure that Mathas' bloodline does not survive—which ultimately means killing you." As if on cue, the memory of his father's order flashed in his mind. *"My father's blood line must die with her. That brother of mine that lives inside her womb must die. Do you understand, Kyren?"* Vaxon had asked.

Kyren shook his head to rid himself of the memory.

"So why save me?" Faeva asked, looking as if she might pass out.

"Listen, Faeva," Kyren hissed. "And get this straight. Despite what you may think of me, I would not willingly murder a pregnant woman. Never. You understand?"

He thought of Ren and little Rya... No more than a few weeks old.

Sparing her a second time? He couldn't do it, not even for Ashyra's sake and the thought broke his heart.

When she left, Kyren almost felt relieved but couldn't. Vaxon would punish Ashyra and this time, there was a chance that he wouldn't be able to convince his father to stop.

The foul, bitter twinge of magic-depletion gas wafted to his nose.

*Great.* That gave him about... two hours before it killed him. *That explains why* *there are magical objects in the caves...*he thought, reflecting back on what Jahad had warned him of before he'd been sent here. *Time to go fetch one of them.*

As he approached the caves, he saw Eiridan, the Healer Wizard, stepping into one of them. With a growl, Kyren mentally cursed himself and formed darkness around himself. He created a powerful spell that formed a wall so that Vaxon could not hear or see them.

It drained his darkness, so he would have to make this quick. He used another spell of darkness to enhance his vision to see into all the caves at once. It drained him even worse because it was one of the more powerful spells he had, so he only left it up for a second. Just long enough to compare the caves' Guardians with each other. What he saw inside Eiridan's shocked him.

As he dropped the enhanced vision spell, Kyren darted inside Eiridan's cave. The Healer Wizard whirled around to face him near the entrance. "Have you come to kill me?" Eiridan asked him. "I'm just here to get the item your father sent me to get."

Kyren shook his head with a dark laugh. "You really need to quit being so naïve. My father wouldn't just leave it lying around in a cave without something or someone to guard it. Think about it... He didn't leave the other supplies lying around unguarded."

"That's fair… So what are you warning me about?" Eiridan frowned.

"You're about to face an Elemental Alpha dragon, one of the original Elementals from the first dragon bloodlines." Kyren really wanted to know what world in the Republic his father had traveled to in order to capture the creature.

"And?" Eiridan pressed.

It irritated Kyren how much Eiridan could see through him. He paused, glaring at the wall, as Kyren pieced together what reasons his father could possibly have with giving Eiridan a dragon more powerful than all the other ones combined. Realization struck him and he blurted the words as quickly as possible. His energy ebbed from the protection wall. "Your dragon is dangerous. More so than the others because my father is angry with me for sparing so many Magi. He's punishing you too since I chose to help you. The dragon that lies beyond the second door into the mountain won't listen to anything you say. Your best bet is to fight or tame it."

Eiridan ran his fingers through his smooth black hair and for once, his young, kind face looked worried. "How would I tame it? I don't know the first thing about dragons."

Kyren shrugged. "I just came to warn you. I'm not going to hold your hand. But a small piece of advice: if you submit to it, there's a chance it may spare you for your courage. It's still likely you'll die."

Eiridan nodded and started to sway. "Wh... Why do I feel so weak?"

Kyren chuckled mirthlessly. "Effects of my father's magic-depletion gas. Get used to it. You only have a few hours before it kills you, unless you get the item he left."

"His games..."

Kyren nodded, lips pressed together in a firm, angry line. "... It's sick, what he's doing."

Eiridan glanced at him as Kyren turned to leave the cave. "Wait... I know why you're doing this."

"Why?" Kyren swallowed. He wasn't even sure why he was doing this.

"Because deep inside you're afraid of your darkness consuming you, of becoming your father."

Kyren gritted his teeth. Saving one Healer Wizard's life didn't make up for the lives he had taken the previous day, or how he had let the darkness get to him. It certainly didn't make up for killing his half-brother and did nothing for the guilt that consumed him. Ashyra would be ashamed and worse; he had failed the Father. Vaxon was getting exactly what he wanted; Kyren turning into a monster before his death.

But Kyren knew better than to play this game with Vaxon. Eventually, he would be caught if he kept saving Eiridan too many times. One day, he would have to kill him and after him, Faeva. The only thing he could hope for was to die before that day came.

"You're the only one who's tried to see passed who my father is. To see passed the darkness in me," Kyren muttered.

"Thank you for saving us at the cave. And for warning me now."

Eiridan's voice stayed with him as he sprinted out of the cave. He released the dark wall preventing Vaxon from seeing or hearing them and immediately, he collapsed onto the ground with a violent cough. His head spun but he stumbled to his feet and glanced at the caves. Vaxon would see that pause as Kyren trying to regain his strength before facing his own Guardian and that he only let Eiridan go so that he could focus on himself and get the antidote.

With the magic-depletion gas and how much he had used with those two powerful spells, Kyren had no energy to spare. He was going to have to walk wherever he was heading to. Unfortunately, walking proved difficult. His muscles refused to cooperate and it was getting harder and harder for him to breathe. Had Kyren finally pushed himself too far?

After exploring the mountain ranges where the caves were, it was obvious that there wasn't one specifically for him. *Is this how I finally die?* Kyren wondered. The trees started growing thicker but he checked every cave, cavern, or even hole he came across. Every single one of them had already been claimed by another Magi.

Kyren continued on his way, until he emerged from the trees into another clearing. Far to the left was another cavern, but from what he could tell it was already empty. Lying on the ground were Jesyth, Dyrdra, and Erai. It looked as if Dyrdra was dead. Clenching his fists, he knew he didn't have the energy to call darkness to prevent Vaxon from seeing it.

If he let them live…

His children would die.

*Maybe I can give Erai a quick death,* he thought, darting over there. Kyren grabbed Erai by the neck, keeping the boy just in front of him. The magic gas must have depleted his energy because the poor boy was unconscious. *Good,* Kyren thought bitterly. *As least he won't see it coming.*

# DARK MAGI

"Kyren. A boy? You're going to kill a child? Seems low even for you," Jesyth growled.

"Come any closer, and he dies." Did his voice waver? Kyren tightened his grip on the boy to push the thought aside. *Kill him. Just kill the boy and get it over with,* Kyren ordered himself, but his hand refused to move.

"What is your endgame, Kyren? Do you have family who actually cares that you exist?"

He snarled at Jesyth , hiding the fact that the mention of his family brought pain to his chest. "What's it matter?"

"Listen, he has your family right?"

Kyren tightened his grip on Erai.

"No answer means yes. Do you honestly think you're going to make it out of here alive?"

*No,* Kyren thought, but he couldn't say the words out loud.

"Do you really think he'll let your family live after you die?"

His stomach twisted and Kyren felt bile in the back of his throat. *Ashyra. Ren. Rya.* They were his world, more important to him than anything else. Part of him wanted to call upon the Father or His Light for help, but he couldn't...

Not with this.

# JOANNA WHITE

At this point, Kyren's entire body trembled and he blinked back tears. No. Vaxon couldn't see him as weak. He had to do this horrid thing to ensure his family's safety.

With an internal cry of agony, Kyren twisted Erai's head to the side.

Immediately, Erai went limp.

Jesyth slammed gravity toward him, knocking Kyren back. Voices murmured from nearby, so he called darkness around him like a blanket and teleported deeper into the trees closer to the voices. The entire world around him spun from the drain of his teleportation spell as he leaned against a tree, breathing heavily. A dull ache coursed through his body and for a moment, it was almost impossible to move. *Pushing yourself too far,* Kyren thought.

Voices echoed through the leaves, so Kyren forced himself to his feet and waited for the Magi to walk through. Sure enough, branches were shoved aside and Reth walked out into the small clearing.

"You might want to stay away from your brother," Kyren warned, making his tone sound bored, despite how exhausted he was—both physically and emotionally. *Since Vaxon wants Nyk alive, I can't kill Reth yet. He'll use Reth as blackmail to ensure Nyk follows through with his*

**94**

*promise.* Deep inside, he despised how every life in this place was Vaxon's, how it was his to command whether Kyren was forced to kill them, or leave them alive.

He *despised* it.

"What do you want?"

"To warn you. You really hate my family, so I think it would be fair to tell you that Nyk may or may not have ties with my father."

"You're a liar." Reth glared at him and looked as if he wanted to attack.

Kyren stayed where he was, as if the man wasn't even a threat. "And I'm warning you instead of killing you. Your brother has been favored by my parents, and there is a high chance that he will go along with them. If not for himself, then for you."

"You're a liar." Reth growled. "You've killed a lot of Magi already, Kyren. Think you're ready to take me?"

Kyren smirked at him. "Not today. I'm off to save my own skin. The closer you stay to Nyk, the closer you get to my father. Remember that, old friend."

A few miles through the trees, he encountered Penna, Gyra, and Lytti. The plant mage, Lytti, was doing well to fend the metal and earth mage away, so Kyren stopped and watched them for a moment. He knew Vaxon had no interest with any of them, so he waited to do what was expected of him; kill the winner.

Being separated from her allies was Lytti's demise. Gyra yanked earth all around her, closing her in. Kyren ignored the girl's screams, but he couldn't ignore the sickening crunch as she was crushed to death.

Gyra and Penna sighed in relief and took a moment to rest.

Kyren raised his hands, thinking of his next attack. Darkness surged around them like an incoming storm, and rained down needles upon them, piercing their skin multiple times. They collapsed onto the ground, coughing and bleeding until finally, their breath stopped.

Kyren collapsed to the ground, panting. It had been a simple spell, but his magical energy was almost completely gone, not leaving much left to be drained by the magical gas. His vision blurred and his skull pounded, but he blinked several times, struggling to stay awake. Pain like lightning tore through him and he screamed. He could almost hear Jahad or Mathas yelling at him for continuing to overuse his magic.

Just as he fell, a young girl appeared in front of him.

"Did it work?" she asked.

# DARK MAGI

Kyren was so out of it he hadn't realized that she'd cast a healing spell on him. He jumped to his feet and cursed at her. "Stupid girl, do you realize what you've done?" She was too young and too weak— the naïve little fool should have stayed hidden.

Now he would have to kill her, a young girl... No older than fourteen.

"You're weak," he whispered, practically a sob. "You shouldn't have come to me. I don't want to kill you."

"What?"

With a bitter ache in his chest, he looked at her, shocked by her actions. "I hope my daughter turns out to be as kind as you." *If she hadn't have come to me, I could have pretended not to see her. If I don't fight her, then Vaxon will kill Ashyra or Ren and Rya. I—I can't let that happen,* Kyren thought with a sorrowful heart. He had no energy to hold up a magical wall like he did with Eiridan and because of the caves, letting him go had been... excusable.

"I have to kill you." Kyren stood to his feet and glared down at her.

"Kyren, please—"

"I'm so sorry," he choked.

Kyren reached out a hand, prepared to use darkness to drain her instantly, killing her in the quickest way possible. As he did, his hand slammed against something hard.

A shield.

The instant it came up around her, he used darkness to teleport away.

*"Foolish boy!" Vaxon screamed at him, years before. "Always using darkness to hide and teleport away. I did not raise a coward!" With each word, Vaxon brought his hand down, digging dark needles into his skin by the hundreds.*

*Kyren, no older than ten, whimpered. "Father... p—please!"*

*"Enough is enough! I will not raise a coward!"*

The flashback ended almost as soon as it began. Kyren collapsed to his knees, shaking his head to rid himself of the agonizing memory.

Suddenly, gray fog appeared in his hands, dissipating to reveal a scroll.

*Kyren, most of the Magi will not succeed in receiving their items. Even the ones who do will die. Vaxon has cast the spell of Shattered Sight. The instant the living Magi touch their items, they will all become berserkers—creatures that see only evil in others, and it will not stop until the rest of them are dead.*

*You are their only hope of survival. I have gained followers and loyalty out here.*

# DARK MAGI

*With the alliance of the remaining Magi, there just might be a chance for rebelling again. At last, we can overthrow your father and with his demise, finally seek aid from the Republic. Now is the time. Go to the twenty-seventh cavern.*

*There you will face Odahvai—the original black dragon. His three servants guard the necklace that will keep you alive through the gas. I hope it also has the magic power to stop Shattered Sight. Defeat them, and then fight him. You must convince him to side with us. Do whatever you must. After you have Odahvai's loyalty, don't worry. The Magi will all try to escape, using their own magic and knowledge. As they do, Vaxon must believe that you are going to try to stop them, so you must fight them.*

*Make him believe it is real, but then allow them to capture you on the way out, so that you can escape with them. He still has your family and I cannot get to them, not yet. For this reason, he has to believe you are still doing what you can to stop this. Use your darkness to mask whatever tasks you must accomplish to finish this. If you suspect any of them are loyal to Vaxon... warn their friends and allies.*

*Here is the information on Odahvai's three servants. I wish you the best of luck, nephew.*

# JOANNA WHITE

-        *Jahad.*

It was written in the Forbidden Tongue, one Kyren knew Vaxon couldn't read and what was even more genius was that it was spelled to be invisible. To Vaxon who was no doubt watching him, Kyren was simply staring out into space to rest... Not reading a secret scroll from his uncle.

As soon as he had read the letter from Jahad, he burned it, just in case the invisibility spell wore off. He formed his dark fire to look as if he was burning brush to walk through.

*Dragons. Odahvai.* His mind reeled, immediately calculating all he had to do.

Two hours to live—well, about an hour now. An hour to reach the caves, fight Odahvai's three servants, and convince the ancient black dragon to side with them.

Kyren shook his head. *Thanks, Jahad. Leaving me the hard part.*

With that, he began the long walk to the caves, rather than teleporting. He needed to save as much of his energy as he could, for facing Odahvai.

Entering the dark cave, he drew some of the darkness into himself, giving him extra energy and recalled the information on Odahvai's three servants.

*Acid is the only thing that penetrates their scales, so it would have to be a spell of*

# DARK MAGI

*acid. Odahvai only cares for ancient spells, so to impress him, I must use one of my oldest. All three servants must be killed at once since their lives are bound together. That leaves me with only one choice for a spell and it's one that could very well kill me,* Kyren thought.

He strolled out into the massive cavern at the center of the cave. Odahvai huffed, flaring fire and darkness from his nostrils. "Mage of Darkness. Come. Fight my servants... If you are still alive afterward, perhaps we can talk about what you want."

Kyren wasn't surprised that the original dark dragon had already read his thoughts. Dragons were mysterious and powerful creatures, with powers beyond human understanding.

The three servants—each a smaller black dragon—stepped forward and each one was elongated and bony. Only one had wings, but they were battered and littered with holes. The second had spikes all over his body. The third was the scrawniest of the three. She opened her mouth and flaming balls of darkness hurled toward him.

Kyren raised his hands, forming a wall of darkness that stretched from the ground to the cavern's ceiling. With a grunt, he threw his hands forward, shooting it

# JOANNA WHITE

toward the three dragon-servants. As they tried to escape, he formed it into a circle so that they were surrounded. His hands shook with effort, and sweat coated every inch of his skin. He could feel his body beginning to tire. *I'm going to... kill myself with this spell. But I have to. It's an ancient and dark spell, one that has to impress Odahvai. If it doesn't... I'll die.* It was a foolish strategy, but it was all he had.

They prodded against his dark wall, but it never wavered. It drew closer to them, consuming them, eating their bodies away like acid.

When there was nothing left of them, Kyren collapsed, as his body lulled into a deep sleep.

*Vuloor.*

*Darkness...*

*Vuloor. Raan sii ka hai. Eriliin oknau sii, gehv.*

*Darkness. Feel it inside you. Draw upon it, yes.*

*Kur dai.*

*Take mine.*

*Hai lus Ulurkaan, tai hai lo ahkra vo Dovan.*

*You are powerful, yet you have the courage of a Dragon.*

*Ah rak dahriz, Yu'u fai niik hai.*

*For this reason, I will help you.*

# DARK MAGI

*Neh kur dir vuloor. Bahn sii wak agnai hai ahn Ulurkaai hai.*

*Now take my darkness. Use it to fuel you and empower you.*

Slowly, blackness turned to white as Kyren awoke. Odahvai towered over him, his scales obsidian black, twinkling like a thousand stars in the nighttime sky. He was at least fifty to eighty feet long, with a powerful snout that huffed darkness when he breathed.

Somehow, Kyren's strength had returned. A necklace rested over his heart, allowing darkness to course from it, into him. "This is your energy?"

Odahvai snorted, making smoke and darkness flare from his nostrils. *"Gehv.* Yes. I have implanted a part of my own energy into the *Luhaar kol*—how you would say in your tongue, magical necklace."

Kyren calculated the time in his mind, and as he sensed the air, he knew the gas was gone. "The Magi will all be trying to escape now. I have to keep up appearances... Make Vaxon believe I'm trying to fight and stop them, yet I have to let them capture me." Kyren cursed; it went against everything he stood for—letting someone beat him in a fight.

*"For dri hai reh zo Yu'u?* What do you need of me?" Odahvai asked.

"I'm going to need your help shutting the anti-magic shield down. It's powered by Wessi herds."

"*Lak tor wak Yu'u.* Leave that to me."

Kyren smiled. Dragons weren't made of magic, but they could harness the oldest form of it. The shield, being anti-magic, would not affect his ability to fly out of it. It would be a simple task for Odahvai to fly out, kill the Wessi herds, and power down the shield. All Kyren had to do was pretend to fight the Magi until they took their chance to escape, and then allow himself to be captured by them as they left.

*Easy,* Kyren thought sarcastically.

He clenched his hands into fists, feeling dark power surge through him, making his blood pump.

Grinning, he formed a plan in his mind. Briefly, his thoughts drifted to his family. All he could do was hope and pray they would live. *If not,* he thought, *I'm doing the right thing. As soon as we rebel and I kill Vaxon, if they're dead, I'll quickly join them.*

Odahvai inclined his head toward him. *"Neh tii dir fehrdai, wak kahllrai tor sor mai rel."*

# DARK MAGI

Without waiting for a translation, Kyren left the cavern. He already knew what the words meant:

*Now go, my friend, to the freedom that awaits us all.*

## CHAPTER EIGHT

ODAVAI'S ROAR REVERBERATED throughout the entire area. The sound sent shock waves through each and every creature, carried through the wind across the plains and grasslands, across the snowy tundra, around every nook and cranny. It shook the ground underneath Kyren's feet in time with his pounding chest. *"Kahllrai sor mai!"*

*Freedom is upon us.*

*Now is the time,* Jahad's voice called inside his mind.

Mind-telepathy was easily tracked, so it had to be brief, and it was hard to cloak. If Jahad was to keep his betrayal to Vaxon a secret, then Kyren would not be able to reply.

Part of Kyren felt bad for not replying but it would be too dangerous as he thought over the words of Jahad's letter.

# DARK MAGI

*Most of the Magi will be escaping. Father will expect me to stop them, otherwise he'll kill Ashyra, Ren, and Rya.* The thought of being forced to kill even more of his own kind—to spill even more innocent blood—made Kyren feel as if he had just swallowed acid.

But to save his family, he would do anything. *Father will find out about the Magi's escape. Odahvai is taking care of the Wessi herds, but I have to prepare in case Father has a back-up plan. Which he always does. He'll ensure that I die here. I have to find a way to escape without him figuring it out.*

*After I ensure my loyalty to him first.*

Kyren shoved his emotions deep inside himself until they were locked away where he couldn't reach them. As he closed his eyes, he called darkness to him, not in the form of magical energy, or in the form of power, but inside his mind. He used it to cloud himself, until it shadowed his morals, hesitations, and emotions, until there was nothing left of him but darkness and his mission.

Immediately, three names of Vaxon's highest Magi targets popped into his mind—the names of those that Vaxon wanted dead the most—the ones that were supposed to have died in the bloodbath and lived. Morko, Savah, and Faeva.

The moon overhead was slowly being covered, turning vermillion in color. *Blood moon.*

Off in the distance, wolves howled, sending chills scuttling down Kyren's spine. His necklace flashed the same color that the moon was turning, as if the necklace itself was bleeding. A strange sensation overcame him, a feeling pricking at his mind with tiny needles. The darkness inside him quickly squelched it, but he recognized the feeling well:

*Shattered Sight.*

*I thought my necklace stopped it?* As he looked down at the bleeding-necklace, Kyren gritted his teeth. Apparently, Vaxon had found a way around even that. No matter what he did now, the spell would begin soon.

He would have to hurry then.

Darting off into the trees near the Heart Tree, he ran as fast as his legs could carry him. It wasn't long before the air around him stirred.

Kyren whipped around to stand-face-to face with Morko, the Air Mage. "Well, Air Mage, looks like this is your unlucky night." Kyren grinned, sending dark particles into the air.

# DARK MAGI

Morko waved his hands, forming it into a medium-sized cyclone between them. But Kyren's dark particles were already there. The more Morko forced the wind around him and drew it toward himself for energy, the more that Kyren's dark particles landed on him.

Morko knew nothing of this. The particles were too tiny to see. One instant, he was sending wave after wave of air toward Kyren, who blocked it with a dark shield, and the next, Kyren felt a surge of power as his particles touched Morko's skin.

Kyren clicked his tongue. "Gotcha." He jerked his hands out like claws, thinking the command, and the darkness obeyed. The particles embedded into his skin. Within three seconds, Morko's skin grayed and his veins turned black.

By the fourth second, he was lying on the ground in a pile of ashes.

Kyren felt energy leave him, but the necklace soon replenished it. He didn't stop to revel in the power that it gave him. No, he simply moved on, using his powers over darkness to quickly track his next target and teleport to them. With the extra energy, he had enough to almost fight his father head-on with magic.

Almost.

# JOANNA WHITE

With the necklace, he was on a completely different level than the other Magi here. They had no idea just how weak they were compared to him.

Compared to Vaxon.

Savah was riding on a Pegasai, who had strayed from the herd, heading toward the mountains closest to the Pegasai fields. Kyren teleported onto a branch toward the top of a tree ahead of where they were flying.

Neither could see him.

He waved his hands, thinking *Dark Cloud.* Immediately, his darkness swirled around them, blocking out light. The Pegasai whinnied at the loss of sight. Kyren pressed his hands together, manipulating the darkness to throw the Pegasai and Savah out of the sky. He teleported to the ground and ensured both of their necks had broken.

The power inside him locked away his emotions and kept him from being haunted by her animalistic screams. Heroes wouldn't slaughter innocent people. How many great Magi had fought evil dictators like Vaxon before him, how many had risked their lives, or lost loved ones because they refused to give in? How many Magi had faithfully served the Father and His Light, had courageously stood up to save the world as they knew it, no matter the cost?

# DARK MAGI

Not Kyren.

He couldn't. His whole life had been filled with pain. Without Ashyra and his children... He loved them too deeply. It seemed impossible for him to do any actions that could result in getting them killed. How did the heroes of old do it? How did they just let their family members die, even if it was for the right cause? Kyren couldn't do it. He couldn't make himself do it.

Maybe his plan to fool Vaxon would work. After these few kills to impress his father, maybe Vaxon would believe it. All of the people he had killed would haunt him for the rest of his life, but he simply could not disobey. Anyone could hate him for it, but not when it came to his wife and children— innocent children.

As Kyren jumped down from the tree, he felt a familiar tingling presence from behind him.

Vaxon.

"I'm surprised. I expected you to attempt to escape with them." Vaxon's gaze was emotionless as he met Kyren's.

Kyren shrugged, but kept his expression just as impassive. "I've already accepted that I'm going to die here. I just want to make sure before you find a way to kill me that I've done my part to keep Ashyra and our children alive."

Vaxon harrumphed. "It will take more than killing two inferior and yet troublesome Magi to impress me, Kyren." He nodded his head to the back of the room, where Ashyra had been chained to a post. The wound on her shoulder still bled while Ren clutched Rya tightly at her feet.

One Nires guard stood behind his wife with the same tool as before and he continued peeling the flesh from her bones. Ashyra's screams tore through him and Kyren darted toward the image, as if he could make his father stop.

"I'll kill Faeva and the other Magi I see. I'll destroy them all, Father. I won't fail you," Kyren blurted. "I'll become the son you want me to be."

Vaxon raised his hand and the Nires stopped.

Ashyra's body sagged as her blood dripped to the floor, barely missing their children.

Tears fell from his eyes like waterfalls but he met his father's cruel gaze and held it. "I'll embrace the darkness." Kyren's shoulders sagged, as he finally surrendered.

"We will see."

With that, his father's magical projection disappeared.

# DARK MAGI

Heart heavy and in utter agony, Kyren choked and teleported away. His magical levels were barely depleted, so he still had plenty left to kill his next target before teleporting to his last.

Cavyr, the Space Wizard, was with a group of centaurs and Minotaurs attempting to climb the mountain to reach the shield.

The moment Kyren popped up in front of him, Kyren snarled in fury, fury at the situation, at Vaxon, at his darkness, at everything. "Did you honestly think that I would allow you to escape?"

Cavyr appeared unafraid of him, but he waved his hand, throwing a portal behind Kyren.

Knowing that Space Wizards loved the whole throw-a-portal-behind-you-and-attack-you-from-behind trick, Kyren ducked forward, before wrapping his darkness around him.

He teleported behind Cavyr. "How much you want to bet that you *don't* like your own trick used against you?" Kyren asked.

By the time Cavyr turned around, Kyren had already slammed his fists against him. The Space Wizard reeled from the blow, but portaled away. No. Ashyra could not afford any more Magi to live or escape him.

# JOANNA WHITE

Kyren could not fail.

*I'll embrace the darkness,* he had promised.

Now, it was time to keep it and ensure his family's safety. Kyren closed his eyes, using his darkness to help him sense where the *good* was coming from. To do this, he truly had to let darkness inside the deepest parts of his soul, allowing it to consume him. He had to be truly evil, in order to sense the good in others. It burned him like a wild flame, but it enabled him to locate Cavyr quickly. More than that, he had to fully let the darkness in so that he could do what he needed to do in order to act as if he was on Vaxon's side, when in reality, the stronger Magi would escape and join Jahad in the rebellion. Without the darkness inside him, Kyren might have thought about the cost of such a thing—how many lives had been taken to rebel against Vaxon? But the darkness clouded his mind, closing him off from the light.

Just as Cavyr popped up far to Kyren's right, he formed a spear of darkness and threw it at the Space Wizard. Cavyr collapsed as he bled out, muttering something about someone named Hylo.

Kyren winced and teleported to his last target.

Faeva.

**114**

# DARK MAGI

"Kyren, there you are! How exactly does your uncle expect us to break free of the barrier? I know you're hesitant to help us, but come on you have to have a way—"

Kyren formed darkness around her, putting her into a deep sleep. Her body collapsed onto the ground, and he closed his eyes and let the spell simply shut her mind down. It was the most painless and peaceful way to kill her. He could almost imagine her protesting if she were awake, saying how much she had trusted him and doubted he could kill a pregnant woman.

Tears fell from his eyes and the pain and guilt of what he had done was strong enough to shatter the darkness in his soul. He collapsed on all fours, holding her head gently in his lap as her breathing stopped. It was the only way to prove to Vaxon he was still on his side, the only way to ensure that Jahad's rebellion went unnoticed and unsuspected, the only way to keep Ashyra safe. Part of Kyren knew he should not have shown such weakness as to cry and mourn for Faeva when Vaxon was watching but he had no control over his body any more. Kyren's entire body trembled, rocking back and forth as he held Faeva to his chest tightly.

His only prayer was that Vaxon believed him.

# JOANNA WHITE

Kyren looked up, knowing that the creatures Vaxon used as spies were out there. "Well?" he choked, glaring up at the sky in fury and pain.

Vaxon's form appeared in front of him. "That—*brother* of mine that resided inside her womb is dead and with him, Mathas' bloodline. You've done well, my son. Soon, you will be allowed to die and this will all be over."

Kyren wanted to wince at the word, but he remained perfectly stoic. Desperately, he stared at the magical projection, hoping for a glimpse of his wife. Ashyra had been unchained and lay on a cloth mat beside their children. "She'll be safe?" he asked, holding back a sob.

Vaxon nodded and the projection disappeared.

Wrapping darkness around him, he collapsed against a tree, putting his face into his hands. He called darkness to him in a form Vaxon would recognize as drawing it to him to increase his energy levels.

In reality, he just wanted to be alone. Away from the world around him, away from the Magi, away from his father, away from everyone. He collapsed onto the ground, knees shaking, body trembling, and threw up what little remained in his stomach.

# DARK MAGI

Then he stood up, pulled darkness inside him and thought: *Dream Telepathy.* He pushed invisible darkness away from him, from his mind to Eiridan's. Kyren explained the situation to him as quickly as possible and told him of the plan for them all to safely escape.

*"Wait! Kyren?" The foolish Healer Wizard tried to continue the conversation further.*

*Kyren just wanted to be left alone. "I'm still here... What do you want?"*

*"Why isn't the wand helping me? Your father said it would..."*

*"My father is a liar, Eiridan," Kyren said, thinking to how his father seemed so proud about how he killed Faeva, and yet...*

*Vaxon was still going to try to kill him.*

*He hadn't killed her to save his own life, but to convince Vaxon that he was obedient and not helping the Magi rebels, to convince Vaxon that nothing suspicious was going on so that Jahad's rebellion had a chance of destroying his father once and for all. Still, the thought that his father, no matter how proud he was of Kyren, wanted him dead, stung. Then again, the sadistic man was only proud of him for doing something utterly deplorable.*

# JOANNA WHITE

*Kyren tore himself from his thoughts to try to hurry the conversation along. "By now you should know that the spell might be gone, but your dragon was a particularly nasty breed. One that is able to make it harder for other magical creatures to heal. I just hope you survive it. It's just like my father to destroy everything good..." Kyren cleared his throat and pressed on. "We won't have long before my father figures out what we're doing and tries to stop us. Make it count. I have to go. Don't make me sorry I told you." Kyren already regretted telling Eiridan. He felt as if he had told him too much.* He's just going to betray you to Vaxon, and then everything you just did will have been for nothing, a voice whispered in the back of Kyren's mind.

*"I won't... Kyren?"*

*"What?"* Kyren asked, as he thought, Just go away!

*"I've always been your friend..."*

Friend. Deep inside, he didn't even truly understand what the term meant. It was empty. Meaningless.

The way Eiridan looked at him in their minds, as if he was a wounded dog who had been beaten too many times, a lost puppy who had no idea where to go or what to do.

# DARK MAGI

*I just killed four innocent people, and one of them was pregnant! I killed her! I don't deserve your pity!* Kyren screamed internally, but kept Eiridan from hearing it. All he said was, *"Stop looking at me like that, then."*

*"Like what?"*

*"With pity. You think I'm broken. You think you can fix me, don't you?"*

*"No. I don't. I see that now. The Father is the only one who can fix your problems and give you forgiveness if you seek it. I'm just here to help and listen. Friends do that, you know."*

Kyren looked away. *"Do they?"* He couldn't believe that the Father would ever forgive him for what he had done. Ever.

*"The real ones do."*

*"Whatever,"* Kyren snapped. *"You better go back to your girlfriend. She needs you."*

*"And you don't? Anyway, when I wake up, I'll just go back to my prior state of discomfort."*

*"No, I don't need you. And anyway, you're already awake, and you have been for a while. I'm keeping you here to tell you what you need to know without my father finding out. It's draining me, so goodbye."* With that, he dispersed the spell.

# JOANNA WHITE

He couldn't help but think back to Eiridan's words. *The Father is the only one who can fix your problems and give you forgiveness if you seek it. I'm just here to help and listen. Friends do that, you know.*

*No, the Father can't help me or forgive me, Eiridan. No one can. You don't want to—no, you can't help a monster like me.*

A piercing screech shattered the silence of the night and pulled him from Eiridan's mind, out of the dream telepathy spell. It was inhuman, and the sound made Kyren wince. His necklace pulsed and burned his skin. He glared at it, just as the red-color pulsed and thumped, like a beating heart, until it was still. Crimson faded away, until it was just as dull as it had been before. Kyren looked up at the moon, fully red now. Somehow, he knew.

Odahvai was dead.

*No,* Kyren wanted to scream. Instead, he stared out into the forest around him, heart racing in his chest, fists trembling. Odahvai... How had his father done it? Had Odahvai died by a mere accident, or something more? Something Vaxon caused? The unanswered questions plagued Kyren and grief threatened to overtake him. Hopelessness weighed as heavy as the guilt of what he had done. If an ancient creature as powerful as Odahvai had failed, then what chance did they have? The dragon had saved his life and like everything and everyone who ever helped Kyren, Odahvai had paid the ultimate price.

Kyren would always be alone. Ashyra and his children had been all he'd ever had but even now, he was losing them. He could feel them slipping and fading away from him, just like everyone else in his life had.

Just like Odahvai.

Exhaling sharply, Kyren tried to force away his thoughts and focus back on the task at hand. Pulling darkness around him, Kyren teleported to the top of the mountain and looked all around him. The anti-magic shield was still there. Desperately, he glared at the moon once again. Now that it was completely full, Shattered Sight would begin. If Odahvai was dead, it meant that Kyren's necklace no longer worked. It sent out waves of a counter-spell to stop Shattered Sight, but without it…

Everyone inside the arena would turn on each other.

The arena instantly responded. The forest shook and trees trembled and collapsed from the sheer number of furious herds attacking and killing each other.

Above him, Phoenixes flew, flapping their wings, spreading fire atop the trees. A Pegasus collided with another, and the two furiously attacked back-and-forth, biting and kicking. Out of seemingly nowhere, a griffin charged toward them, clawing at the Pegasus as it did. Bright cobalt blue blood sprayed onto the world below.

Smoke billowed away from the trees that were on fire. A Minotaur charged into a centaur, slicing at the half-human with its axe. Kyren looked away from the blood and gore, gagging.

As he looked back at the shield, a group of Magi fought nearby. The air around them whirled, with the combined efforts of Enya and Eriswen, using their air and shields to protect as many Magi from the spell as they could.

Kyren found Eiridan, who was beside Jaeyria. She charged toward Kyren, using her shadows to chain him down.

Laughing as a show for Vaxon, Kyren shattered them and chained her with his own. Before he had a chance to do anything, the oxygen inside his body was being depleted. Enya met Eiridan's eyes and nodded.

*Obviously, she's in on this.* Kyren was losing oxygen fast. *You have to make it believable! Not this quick!* Switching his tendrils from heading toward Jae, he caught Enya in their grasp, pinning her body down, pulling her energy out of her and into himself, draining her. She screamed and collapsed onto the ground.

Eiridan met his gaze with a fearful one. "Kyren, stop this!"

*"It has to be believable,"* Kyren thought to him. *"Remember the plan."*

In his mind, Eiridan hesitated. The idea was beyond cruel, and there was no way he would ever do that to another human being—not even to Kyren.

Kyren growled at him internally. Between the telepathy and draining Enya, as well as holding the others at bay with a dark shield, his levels were depleting fast, especially now that Odahvai's energy was gone from the necklace. *"Curse you, Healer. Just do it! The only way Vaxon will believe I lost is if many Magi work together to team up against me! It's the only way to beat me, and it's the only way to beat him, which is why it's the only way this will work."*

Eiridan still didn't want to.

*"Odahvai is dead and he didn't destroy the shield. You need to follow the plan to take care of me and once I'm out, use your healing magic and combine it with Dyrdra's. Between the both of you, you'll have enough power to cleanse everyone of*

*Shattered Sight. When they're in their right minds, gather the Elves. They can stand beside each other and cast the spell Iced World."*

Eiridan wondered what Iced World was. He had never heard of it before.

*"A powerful spell that only ancient creatures have the ability to cast. It has the power to freeze magical energy. You'll all have to lend them power, but it will freeze the shield. Only when the shield has turned completely to ice do you attack and use every creature you can ally with, every power you can think of. It will take* all *of the remaining Magi and most of the creatures to completely shatter it. But once it's down, you won't have time or energy, but the Wessi herds still have to be killed. That's why you're going to have to call upon the vampires and the werewolves. Convince them with the offer of freedom and they'll join you. They'll kill the Wessi herds while the rest of you recover. Oh and don't forget to lock me in anti-magic chains, or Vaxon will know I can just break free. The Elves should have some."*

Eiridan struggled to process the information all at once.

*"Now, repeat it back to me to make sure you all understood, and before you ask,*

*yes, when I do this I can read your mind. Hurry up, I'm losing energy fast."*

By the time he repeated it all, Enya had collapsed onto the ground, alive and awake, but severely out of it. Jaeyria and Reth had charged at him with real weapons, realizing that magic wouldn't work.

Kyren's eyes lost their pupil and became pitch black. Shadows surrounded him until his true body couldn't be seen behind them. It looked as if his body was made out of dark fog. "I can't let any of you escape!" he hissed. Inside, power surged through his veins and the darkness whispered to him. He had to do it this way to make Vaxon believe he was stopping them, no matter the cost to himself. His family was all that mattered.

By doing his most powerful attack, none would walk away alive. Vaxon would recognize the stance and the spell in his eyes. In doing it, the spell would kill him. Vaxon would get everything he wanted.

Even if Eiridan pulled off the plan and stopped him, the darkness would consume him.

In a way, Eiridan would save him, not just by capturing him and helping him escape from the arena, but by bringing him back and saving him from darkness—from evil and corruption itself.

# JOANNA WHITE

*"Bring me back, Eiridan,"* Kyren whispered to his mind.

"What, Kyren?" Eiridan asked out loud. To the other Magi, it seemed as if he was questioning the same thing they were:

What horrible spell he was about to do.

*Consumption!* Energy surged through his veins, and every inch of his body was hyper-aware of all that was going on. The Magi around him instantly fell to their knees, weighed down by the sheer pressure of darkness around them. Wherever it touched them, it burned, and drained away their very lives and souls.

*"Now! Before I kill them all Eiridan!"* Kyren shouted at him in his mind.

After a brief moment of hesitation, Eiridan nodded. "Eriswen!" Eiridan yelled, "Shield as much as his dark spell as you can! Jae, Nyk, combine your vines and shadows to chain him down! Enya do what you did before. Shara, use your light to expel his darkness, and then wrap him in light."

"How do you know…?" Jae started.

"Just do it!"

Shadows and vines wrapped around Kyren, pinning his ankles and wrists down to the ground, but it didn't stop his magic. He felt air leave his body, but he could hold

# DARK MAGI

his breath for at least three minutes before he passed out. Light fell all around him, blinding him. He closed his burning eyes to try to stop it. The acrid smell of smoke filled his nostrils, and he heard more voices, probably from other Magi. *The fire mage girl and her brother,* Kyren thought.

Vaxon would expect him to try to counter it. He threw his darkness around them in a furious hurricane, whipping it around them so quickly that none of them could stand up.

Eiridan threw his hands out and used a spell to empty Kyren's body of Mathanos. Immediately, Kyren's energy fled him. His darkness slowed, until it stilled altogether. Eiridan stopped, thinking he had done it. Kyren's pupil returned, but then his eyes flashed back once again, and dark fog swirled around him. *"More, Eiridan! You have to drain more!"*

*"Kyren, it could kill you!"* Eiridan mentally shouted.

*"If it does, at least my family will live. The spell is still going and I can't stop it. You have to. Just do it, Healer!"*

His energy drained out of his body, his heart, and his soul. Fatigue and exhaustion slammed into him as agony swept over him in rough currents. He didn't even have the energy to open his eyes, let alone move. Blackness consumed his vision and his thoughts, and his mind began to drift. The dark fog around him finally stilled.

As the last of his energy left his body and was drawn into Eiridan, Kyren faintly smiled. *"Remember the plan, Healer. Escape the arena. Find freedom."*

"What are you doing? He was trying to kill us!"

"I don't care! He had a family just like we do! Vaxon was using him too. I will not kill him. I know what we need to do to break through the barrier," Eiridan responded.

"I'll help," came a response from the young girl healer.

The last thing Kyren heard before he faded into unconsciousness was Eiridan and Dyrdra's voices. "Don't die on me, Kyren."

"Come on! Live!"

*I don't deserve to…*

*"Don't die on us!"*

*Death,* Kyren thought, *would be a sweet thing. A sweet thing indeed.*

# DARK MAGI

## CHAPTER NINE

WHEN KYREN AWOKE, every inch of his body was in agony. He lay on a cot inside a tent. As his eyesight slowly returned after being blinded from Shara's light, Kyren didn't even try to sit up. Between casting the spell Consumption, what the Magi did to team up against him, and then Eiridan draining his Mathanos, it would be awhile before he could move.

Many times in his life Kyren had seen death as the only way to freedom. How many times had he tried to use dark spells to overdo it, to kill himself? How many times had he formed a dark sword and thought of stabbing it into his own stomach?

When he had first been ordered to obey Vaxon and help him find the Magi, Kyren thought about killing himself so that he wouldn't be forced to kill any of the Magi. Then he thought of Ashyra, Ren, and little Rya, who was only an infant. If he killed himself, Vaxon would kill them. Perhaps Ashyra would be with the Father's Light. But Kyren? He couldn't believe the Father's Light could redeem him, even before the Magi had been captured. He would never see her again and that thought haunted him.

And what of Ren and Rya? They were so young, with their whole lives ahead of them. How could Kyren condemn them to death by killing himself?

He couldn't. So he had done the most unspeakable, horrible acts to keep his wife and children alive, doing what most people would never be able to do. The thought that he was just like his father terrified him, but Kyren had shoved it all aside and done what needed to be done.

Now, his final spell should have killed him. He had hoped it would, despite the consequences. Kyren deserved death, wanted it, and craved it, even. Perhaps the Magi and Jahad could rebel, and Ashyra and his children would be saved.

*"Father,"* Kyren mentally prayed, *"forgive me. Save my family."*

"I heard the tale of what happened when you escaped the arena," a voice said, yanking him from his thoughts.

"Jahad," Kyren mumbled.

# DARK MAGI

"I am proud of you, Kyren." His uncle stood at the edge of his cot, looking tall with broad shoulders and a kind expression.

Kyren swallowed, and his skin crawled. The only time anyone had ever been remotely close to being proud of him was when he had killed Faeva.

Jahad obviously sensed his unease and placed a hand on Kyren's shoulder. "You made the right choice, Kyren. You've done it; you're free."

*I'll never be free,* Kyren thought. Instead he asked, "Where are we?"

"In my camp. I've gathered an army to bring down your father once and for all."

Kyren lifted an eyebrow. "You gathered an army already?"

Jahad nodded. "Many people were just waiting for the right moment to strike against Vaxon." After a brief pause, he continued. "I'm going to meet with Vaxon and keep up appearances so he doesn't get suspicious of my involvement."

Kyren frowned and shook his head. "No. He'll see right through you."

Jahad placed a hand on Kyren's chest. "I know how to handle my brother, Kyren. All will be well. Do you need anything before I leave?"

"I'm just going to rest, Jahad."

Jahad nodded, gave Kyren a short smile, and walked out.

Why was it so hard for Kyren to be around his uncle? Was it because Jahad reminded him so much of his grandfather, Mathas? Was it the kindness and forgiveness in his eyes, always ready to forgive Kyren and give him the benefit of the doubt?

*I killed Faeva,* Kyren thought. Even though he had no other choice because he couldn't let his family die, it still haunted him. Maybe he didn't want Jahad around because deep inside, he was terrified eventually his uncle would see him for the monster he really was.

When the messenger came to deliver the news of Jahad's capture, Kyren jumped off the cot and stormed outside. He had no magic energy, yet darkness swirled around his ankles. There was no trace of blue in his eyes at all. They, like he, were consumed with darkness.

Pain pounded against his body, but it was not a physical pain. No, it was the sort of agony that oozed its way into Kyren's soul, mixing with the darkness in a twisted harmony, one that plagued his thoughts and haunted his mind. It ripped apart everything he had been—the kindness that had started to form inside him for a few Magi friends—

until there was nothing left of him, nothing except the blackness that Vaxon had created.

Lost in his thoughts, Kyren wandered, not caring where in Elloyn he was. Memories of Jahad training Kyren as a young boy, playing with him… Jahad secretly marrying Kyren and Ashyra; he had always been there. He had been there to comfort Kyren the night Ashyra had their first child. He had been there when they had their second. All those nights alone in the prison, Jahad came to see him. It was Jahad who would come to him after Vaxon's horrid torture sessions. When Kyren's body had been battered and broken, Jahad had been there. He had cleaned all the blood, had held him through the shakes and seizures, had kept Kyren from going insane in all those long weeks isolated in pitch darkness.

Jahad had been there through it all.

Now…

Now he was in Vaxon's clutches. Just like Ashyra. Just like adventurous young Ren, and fragile little Rya. *He's taken everything from me,* Kyren thought. Hopelessness and despair wrapped around him like a winter cloak, only it was one he couldn't remove.

Kyren stared at the entrance to the camp with a longing in his gaze. Just as he took one step toward it, a voice stopped him.

# JOANNA WHITE

"You can't just *leave*," the voice furiously hissed. It was Eriswen, the Shield Wizard. "I have friends in there too, Kyren. They're all I have left, and I don't want to see them die any more than you want to see your family die. If I can put that all aside to fight your father, you can get your head out of the clouds and fight him too. You're our best hope of getting in there and making a difference. You can't just walk away from that."

"Do you know how much a family means to me, Eris? You don't give up on family, and you never, ever put them in harm's way. I can't let my family down, and I refuse to put them on the butcher's block just to join your *doomed* rebellion." Pretending to be captured by them was one thing; actually helping them lead a war against him was an entirely different story and a risk he was unwilling to take with his family. Kyren clenched his fists, as anger boiled through his blood. Eris... was a *child* compared to him. What did she understand about family? Sure, she had a family full of dragons, and one of them died, but she wasn't married. She didn't know what it was like to be a husband—to be a father.

*Kyren walked into the slave's room down in the basement of the palace, looking for Ren but he was nowhere to be found.*

# DARK MAGI

*Panic tore through him like a raging storm. "Ren? Ren?" His voice rose in fear and his first thought was that Vaxon had changed his mind and decided to kill him.*

*Ren giggled.*

*The sound reached Kyren's ears, warming his heart in an instant, and soothing his terrified soul. Kyren glanced up to where the sound had come from to see Ren standing on top of a wooden pillar that was the only thing holding the slaves' quarters upright.*

*"How did you get up there?" Kyren asked, his voice breathless from the worry.*

*Ren shrugged. "Climbed... Hehe."*

*Kyren shook his head but couldn't help the smile that spread onto his face as he reached up to grab his son around the waist.*

*"Papa?" Ren glanced up at him curiously.*

*"Yeah, son? Just don't ever hide like that from me again. You nearly scared me to death."*

*Ren only giggled again but then his expression sobered.*

*"What's wrong?" Kyren sat Ren down on the floor and knelt in front of him so that they were eye-to-eye.*

*Ren's lower lip pouted. "Mommy says she's gonna have 'nother baby. Like me. You'll still love me?" Tears glistened in his bright blue eyes that mirrored Ashyra's.*

*Kyren embraced his son as tightly as he could. "Of course, Ren. You're my son and I'll always love you!"*

*"I'll always love you, too, Papa!"*

Eriswen had no idea what it felt like to put one's family above anything else— above everything else.

She stood in his face, screaming at him as she shoved her hands against his chest. "Do you know what a bond is, Kyren? A bond is the one person that you can fully trust with your safety and well-being. Someone whose magic can effortlessly combine with your own and make both partners close to invincible. And you know what, above all of that, a bond is your family, friend, and the best thing that could ever happen to you. I had a bond, and guess what? I messed up, and I let him die. His family is in Vaxon's dungeons, and if I don't feed Vaxon information, he'll kill them. Most of them are hatchlings. I can't let them die, but that doesn't mean I'm not going to fight Vaxon. If I can still sacrifice after everything that has happened to me, I think you can manage to fight your father."

Kyren slammed her against the tree, eyes flashing coal black in fury. "I know more about a bond than you *ever will, little girl!* A bond is when someone sees through all the evil deeds you commit! When they see the real you that is hidden behind a dozen masks! It's when they love you beyond themselves, when they trust you with their entire being. Family is more than blood, but you always put them before everything. A true sacrifice is sacrificing your own sanity, your *own soul*, for them. Killing innocent people just to keep them alive. Until you've lost everything, until you've been married and understand what it's like to have children of your own, you will never understand, so don't pretend that you do!" With that, he stormed away from her.

He wondered aimlessly, fuming, but he didn't see the creature stalking him.

"Mortal flessssh... Sargon ssssssmells... D-aah-rk Magi! Flessssh..."

Before Kyren could fully respond, he had already been struck. Mentally, he cursed. The speech patterns and accent could only mean one thing:

*Sannurak.* Kyren's body collapsed onto the ground, instantly paralyzed. The *Sannurak* leered above him, its long slender body twisting around him tightly. It had dark green skin, like the inside of a sewer, with three round, beading eyes blinking at him. One rested at the top of its forehead, while the other two were on either side of its face underneath the first eye. Its violet-colored tongue flicked out at him, whipping his forehead. Kyren winced. Cold bit at his skin, spreading across his face like veins.

Panic settled inside his chest, churning his stomach. None of his muscles would work, and by now, the cold had settled on him, preventing him from even using his magic. *It's too late—I can't move or do magic.* If he couldn't kill it, he would die.

Images came, flashing across his mind, quicker than he could fully process them all. Kyren was completely emerged in his memory, lost in his subconscious, lost to reality.

*Kyren dueled against his twin brother. Vaxon stood to the sides, observing the two six-year-old boys in amusement.*

*"Kassan! Attack him while he's vulnerable!" Vaxon glared at Kassan, Kyren's twin, who hesitated.*

*Kyren snarled, and raised his hands until tendrils folded around his twin brother. Kassan grunted and struggled against Kyren's darkness as he pushed against it with his own.*

*Kyren's was stronger—it always had been.*

# DARK MAGI

*When Kyren's tendrils had consumed his brother's, Kassan fell to the ground in a heap.*

*"Get up!" Vaxon hissed.*

*Kyren panted, and his knees wobbled.* No. Do not fall in front of Father, *he thought.*

*Kassan pushed himself up to his feet and tried forming darkness in his hands, but none would come. "I—I'm too exhausted, Father."*

*Vaxon's eyes flashed and black electricity pulsed around him.*

*Kassan flinched.*

*"You... dare to flinch, Kassan?"*

*Fear slithered inside Kyren's heart. Vaxon's voice was absolutely calm, and quiet. Somehow, that was more terrifying than when he yelled.*

*"Kyren," Vaxon addressed him.*

*"Yes, Father?" Kyren somehow managed to keep his voice from shaking.*

*"Use your tendrils to suffocate Kassan."*

*"Th—that will kill him!" This time, Kyren's voice* did *shake.*

*"Now!"*

*Kyren closed his eyes, pulled tendrils of darkness out from his body, and wrapped them around Kassan. The boy struggled and* grunted as the darkness twisted, crushing and compressing his body.

Kyren wanted to stop. He nearly did, but Vaxon had drawn up darkness all around them so that it was pitch black. It brought pain to Kyren's limbs.

"Escape out of his spell, Kassan!" Vaxon urged.

Kassan's eyes flickered black, but he still couldn't form darkness. Kyren could feel it—his brother was completely out of magic energy. "Father, he's... he doesn't have any more magical energy! Please! Can I stop attacking him now?" Kyren choked, desperately trying to hold back a sob.

"No." Agony coursed through the young boy's veins, but he didn't stop his darkness. Kassan continued struggling, but to no avail; Kyren's darkness wrapped around him, consuming him little by little.

"Father, stop this!" a harsh voice rang out.

Suddenly, white light burst around them. Vaxon's darkness was gone, and so was Kyren's. Kassan collapsed onto the ground, unmoving. Kyren's head swam, but he forced himself to stay on his feet. His cobalt blue eyes met his older sister's, who glared at Vaxon in fury.

"Korrah," Vaxon hissed. Korrah had always defied Vaxon and his abuse and

# DARK MAGI

*mistreatment. The fifteen-year-old wasn't afraid to stand up for herself, and especially not for her two younger siblings. Despite their age difference, Kyren had always been close with his older sister—best friends. The only one he ever had.*

*Vaxon hated her. Kyren guessed it was because Korrah was a Light Magi, and a girl, but he never knew for sure.*

*"I won't let you force Kyren to kill Kassan. They're your children!" Korrah screamed.*

*Vassti strolled up behind her. "Korrah, don't..."*

*Korrah ignored her and stepped toward Vaxon, forming a massive ball of light around her. She pushed it out until it exploded around them. The force of the blow forced Kyren to his knees, but when the dust settled, everyone was on the ground except for Vaxon, Korrah, and Vassti.*

*Vaxon cried out in fury, drawing a dark sword to her head. Before Korrah could make a light sword, Vassti jumped in-between them and blocked Vaxon's attack. "I will* not *let you harm my children!"*

*Vaxon grunted and grabbed her waist with darkness.*

*Vassti closed her eyes, and the darkness vanished.*

141

# JOANNA WHITE

*Kyren watched in shock and awe. He had never seen his mother train, but he knew she was powerful. Korrah had told him so.*

*But... powerful enough to stop Vaxon?*

*Vaxon grunted again, as Vassti's eyes snapped open and turned pure white.*

*"Wh...what is she...?" Kyren murmured.*

*Korrah turned to him and tensely smiled. "She's getting into his mind. It's a spell called Morrimine. It allows her to control his actions."*

*Vaxon's eyes became coal black. It was a furious magic battle between them both—white against black. A dark shape formed in front of the sun, blocking out all light. Korrah gritted her teeth, calling a ball of light to her hands. Kyren knew what spell Vaxon was casting. He had heard about it— that only the most powerful Dark Magi could do it.*

*Eclipse.*

*Darkness formed over the sun itself, slithering down to the souls beneath it. The winds picked up and thunder roared, but neither Vaxon nor Vassti moved.*

*"I thought she was controlling him!" Kyren shouted.*

*Korrah shook her head, shouting over the howling wind. "It's hard to get inside someone's mind... She doesn't have complete control—not yet. Just stay back, Kyren!"*

*Kyren refused to move.*

*All at once, darkness exploded, not toward Vassti as they all had been expecting, but toward Kyren.*

*"NO!"*

*Vassti's eyes were still locked in a spell.*

*Korrah darted toward Kyren, shoving him to the ground. "Shield!" To add extra power, she screamed it out loud. Light wrapped around them like a glass blanket, but Vaxon's attack exploded on them.*

*When Kyren woke minutes later, Korrah's body was turned to ashes. Vassti was lying on the ground in a heap. She had lost and had been unable to control Vaxon's mind. The energy she had expended prevented her from doing any more powerful attacks for the rest of her life.*

*Two of her children were dead.*

*Only one child remained; Kyren, the one that Vaxon hated the most. Neither of them could forgive each other and ever since that day, Vassti became an entirely different person who seemed to despise Kyren just as much as Vaxon did.*

# JOANNA WHITE

*Kyren had killed his own brother and had never forgiven himself for it.*

Kyren was jerked from the memory furiously. He had no idea how much time had passed, or even how he was alive.

"It almost killed you," one of Jahad's soldiers said. Kyren couldn't recall the soldier's name, other than he was one of Jahad's spies. "The *Sannurak* had you locked in the memory for about an hour. It had already started eating your energy, and your left leg. We've had our healers do the best they can, but it will be awhile before you can use it."

"By healers you don't mean the Magi, do you?" Kyren secretly hoped they hadn't.

The soldier shook his head. "No. The venom is anti-magic, so the Magi couldn't heal you, anyway. We had a few alchemists tend to it."

"I'm assuming you saved me?" Kyren raised an eyebrow at the man, who nodded. Kyren finally was awake enough to look at his surroundings. He was chained to a tree, but the chains were long enough that he could walk around.

The man walked away.

Kyren's leg burned like fire, but he couldn't move or bend it. Without looking, he could feel that the skin was eaten away, and some of the bone too. His energy was completely gone once again, so he closed his eyes and rested his head against the tree behind him.

Eiridan walked up to him. "What's wrong with you? I thought—I thought things had changed. But your aura, it's—"

"Leave me alone, Healer," Kyren snapped furiously. He glared up at Eiridan as the Healer knelt on the ground in front of him. "Like you care." No one else did. If he was being honest, at this point, Kyren was the one who didn't care. Not about anything except his family, but that only reminded him of the doomed, impossible situation he found himself trapped in.

"I do care, Kyren. What's wrong?"

Kyren was in no mood to speak with anyone, least of all Eiridan. The Healer always did everything to protect others, and his eyes stared at Kyren, constantly looking at him with pity. *I don't need your pity,* Kyren thought.

Anger surged in his chest, fueling the darkness. Or maybe the darkness fueled the anger. Kyren wasn't sure anymore.

All he saw were the images of his worst memory that he'd been forced to relive. He just wanted to be left alone. As if the *Sannurak* was still attacking him, all the faces of the Magi he had killed flashed through his mind.

So, Kyren did what he always did best—pushed everyone away. He tried, at first, aggravating and insulting Eiridan, hoping it would work. "You, for one thing! You're always so placid. No matter what anyone does, you refuse to lash back. You're weak and pathetic, Eiridan! What's wrong with you?"

Eiridan looked at the ground, picking a few blades of grass, still overly calm. It only infuriated Kyren more. "I don't hurt others because it's not right, Kyren."

Kyren shook his head. "You're still recovering from what that dragon did to you. It beat you and you allowed it to!"

Eiridan shrugged. "To be fair, I had no choice. I was weaponless and you told me the dragon might spare me for submitting. It did, so I don't see how this is—"

Kyren growled. "Just shut up. Save it for someone who cares."

Eiridan blinked, hunching his shoulders. Maybe that had finally gotten him. Then, the Healer shook his head. "Look, you clearly did something when you tried to keep your father from finding out what you were doing. The spells you did...

# DARK MAGI

What did it do to you? Is it something I can heal?"

Kyren laughed mirthlessly and it held all the bitterness he felt in his heart. "No. You can't fix anything. In fact, the only thing you ever do is make things worse." The words tumbled out of him before he could stop them. Pushing people away was what he was good at and it was the only thing he had ever known.

Eiridan blinked at him and a wounded expression crossed his face.

Kyren smirked at him but it came out looking more like a grimace. "What's wrong, Healer? Can't handle the truth?" He spat onto the ground in front of Eiridan.

Eiridan stared at him with unshed tears in his eyes.

Kyren scoffed. "What, now you're going to cry? You're pathetic; always have been. Nothing you do ever helps anyone, Eiridan. You're not man enough to stand up when others hurt you, so why would you be man enough to handle the truth?"

That did it.

Eiridan cried out in fury, leapt from his spot in the grass and pounded his fist against Kyren's face. It slammed him back up against the rough bark of the tree, but as Eiridan charged toward him, Kyren snapped his good leg out and nailed the Healer in the chest. He flew backward and sprawled in the dirt, so Kyren charged toward him, using what little maneuvering room the chains gave him to his advantage.

In actuality, he hadn't truly thought Eiridan would snap; it shocked Kyren, but deep inside, Kyren was glad for it. All he wanted was to feel pain, pain that he deserved after everything he'd done.

*Good. He finally realizes that I'm beyond saving.* The chains left room for movement, and the two used their fists to beat each other senseless, even though Kyren limped through most of the fight. Kyren's energy was nonexistent at that point, and his body trembled and shivered. His leg was no doubt getting worse, but he ignored it and the pain from Eiridan's blows.

Eiridan tackled Kyren to the ground and the chains tangled them both. He jabbed his elbow into Kyren's face and that time, he couldn't force his body upright. Eiridan stood, breathing heavily, towering over him as he shouted at him. "I've done nothing but be a friend to you, Kyren Asherex! You're giving into darkness and pushing everyone away, instead of fighting back. Instead, all you're doing is giving up!"

Anger boiled in Kyren's blood, giving him the boost he needed. He swept Eiridan's feet out from under him and

# DARK MAGI

Eiridan's head slammed against the ground with a hard thud. Kyren stumbled to his feet and glared down at him as Eiridan hissed in pain—no doubt from having his breath knocked out. "You have any idea what mistake you made in attacking me, Healer?"

Eiridan's eyes narrowed up at him. "You told me I should stand up for myself," he wheezed.

"Yeah, I did. Guess what? Standing up for yourself is great until you face a stronger opponent." With that, Kyren brought his good leg back and slammed it against Eiridan's chest. Eiridan rolled to the side with another gasp.

Panting from the pain in his own body, Kyren stepped back. The Healer was done for.

Or so he thought.

Instead, to his utter shock and surprise, Eiridan used the tree to stand to his shaky feet. "You know what, Kyren?" Eiridan murmured. There was no anger in his voice, only sadness. "You're no better than your father. I thought you were better. I thought I could help you, even if I'd never be able to reach your father's heart. Well, congratulations, because you've convinced me that I can't help you or anyone in your dark and twisted family! All of you are beyond saving!"

Wasn't that what Kyren had wanted Eiridan to believe? Why then, did Eiridan's words cut him so deeply? "Shut up! You don't know anything about me. Every time I turn around, you're spouting nonsense about how I'm good and that I have redeemable qualities deep inside. You've always been wrong about me, Eiridan, and I'm sick of it. I'm not redeemable and there is nothing in me worth saving!" Kyren screamed, unable to control his words.

Eiridan just stared at him, meeting his gaze for a moment, before he turned around and stormed away.

Erai, the Conjurer kid was standing a few feet away, witnessing the entire thing. "Why can't you be the leader we need?" he whispered softly.

Kyren glared at him. "Go away. I'm not in the mood for you either, kid." Kyren spit blood out of his mouth.

"The army is in disarray after Jahad's capture!" Erai started toward Kyren, but when he glared at him, the kid froze in his steps and briefly shimmered. Kyren didn't think anything of it.

That, of course, only reminded Kyren about what had happened to force him in this mood in the first place. He stumbled to the tree and leaned against it, glaring up at the sky. His father had stolen

# DARK MAGI

everything from him and no matter how hard he had tried, he would never have a normal life or a happy one. What had he done to deserve this? It was as if he had never even been given a chance, as if the odds had stacked against him. Now, Kyren accepted the darkness and his fate.

He would never be free of it.

In Kyren's silence, the foolish kid pressed on. "Do you really think Vaxon'll spare your family? When all of this is over, what do you think will happen to them? I mean, best case scenario he continues to use them as a way to keep you under his thumb," Erai said.

"At least they'll be alive." Kyren's voice sounded empty and dead—exactly how he felt inside.

"Until he doesn't need them anymore. Until they become too much of a threat to keep around."

Kyren sighed heavily. "I'm not about to say that he's honorable. I know as well as anyone that he's killed more innocent people than he can count. But I can't put my family into that type of risk."

"I know that too! Vaxon killed mine! He slaughtered them all!" Tears fell from the kid's face and for once, a pang of sympathy flared in Kyren's chest.

# JOANNA WHITE

"Sorry." The word sounded too small and simple for everything his father had done, for everything *he* had done. "I wish I could fix all of the horrible things my father has done, but I can't change the past. The best I can do is keep him from doing the same to my family."

"No, the best you can do is stop him for good. The best you can do is to help us stand against him." With that, Erai faded away.

Kyren grimaced, suddenly remembering he had killed Erai. A pang of guilt welled in his chest. Was he really hallucinating now?

Despite that, the kid was right, but Kyren couldn't risk his family. He knew what the right thing would be: let Ashyra, Ren, and Rya all die. Sacrifice them for the sake of the world—to overthrow Vaxon.

Kyren *knew* what the right choice would be. But he couldn't.

*"I can't do this anymore, Ashyra..."* Kyren whispered. Vaxon had caught him helping a slave child no older than nine or ten and had killed the boy and made Kyren watch. Then he had brought Kyren back into the torture chamber and left him on the rack overnight in pitch darkness.*

*Ashyra held him in the slave quarters as he cried. It was the first time he had*

**152**

*shown such weakness in front of her, but in that moment, he didn't care. Kyren just wanted to give up, to die. "I am ... more sorry than you'll ever know, Kyren," Ashyra whispered.*

*"I—I try to do what's right and... and it always fails. Every time I do something right, my father ruins it. He destroys everything good. I—I try to be a good man, Ashyra. But being good only gets people killed."*

How many of the slaves had Kyren tried to help only to have them die anyway? All of them. Dozens. Even hundreds, maybe. Enough that Kyren had lost count. Every time he had done something good, Vaxon made sure he regretted it.

*Kyren once walked an old, frail man to his house from the Temple after worshipping the Father and His Son. When Vaxon discovered what he had done, not only did Vaxon order the Temple be burned to the ground, but Vaxon's guards had broken the old man's legs. He had never recovered.*

*A pregnant slave had struggled to carry a heavy pile of clothing the nobles wanted her to wash. She had fallen on the ground, so Kyren had tried helping her stand. At the time, Ashyra had only just told him of her own pregnancy, so he had feared*

**153**

*that she would be like that slave one day. Vassti had seen and informed Vaxon. The pregnant woman had been smothered in the clothes she had dropped on the ground and Vaxon had bought the nobles all new ones for their trouble. After her death, Vaxon had forced Kyren to bury her. "She's dead because of you, Kyren. Because you're trying to be someone you're not."*

*Someone you're not.*

He wasn't good. Every single time he had tried, something horrible had happened and the very person he had tried to help had died. If he tried to help the Magi, they would all die and so would Ashyra, Ren, and Rya.

Why would he help the rebellion and get them killed and lose his family on top of it all? How could he?

Just like that, he turned away from the light. The only way he could allow himself to let thousands of lives to be lost for the sake of his family, was to allow the darkness inside him again.

Darkness wrapped around his mind, fueling the anger once again. *You're a coward, Kyren! You killed your own brother,* Vassti had screamed at him when he was younger. *You killed your own brother, and your sister died to protect you.*

# DARK MAGI

The image warped and changed, until it was Ashyra's voice screaming at him, not Vassti. *"You—you killed so many Magi,"* she choked. *"You killed a pregnant woman, Kyren! Just to save us? I'd rather die than watch you become your father! Because that's exactly what you're doing!"* Though the words weren't a real memory, the mere possibility that they could be, haunted Kyren.

He had pushed everyone away.

Would Vaxon really keep his family alive?

No. It was the hard truth, one Kyren never wanted to face. Not before, not now, not ever. But the fact was that Ashyra, Ren, and Rya were already dead and so was he. Even if by some miracle, his father changed and allowed them to live what would their lives look like?

One by one, the Magi came to him, pleading, begging, yelling at him, trying to change his mind. He was sick and tired of it, tired of them asking him to just *let his family die,* for them. None of them truly cared about his family. If Vaxon killed his children or Ashyra, it would mean nothing to them. Nothing.

As much as he knew that his family would die either way, he had to find a way to save them and helping the Magi would not save them. So, he had no reason to help them. None at all.

Back and forth he went, internally arguing with himself. The war within him was mentally exhausting, taking its toll on his already wounded and weakened body. Hopelessness and despair threatened to force him to just give up. They whispered to him, telling him that he and his family were already dead. *There's no way to save them.* Anger and hatred stormed through him, lighting him on fire. Hatred toward Vaxon for all he'd done, anger toward the Magi for their inability to care about his family, utter disgust and loathing toward himself. Guilt and shame weighed on him, breaking his bones, shattering his heart. Agony swelled inside his stomach, churning and twisting it. The emotions warred inside him, warred just like the darkness fought with his consciousness.

Kyren was losing.

Lyva screamed at him next, blaming him for the deaths of all her loved ones. Her words empowered the darkness, and it smiled, taking more and more control of Kyren. Ever-so-slowly, Kyren was pushed back, locked inside a cage, chained inside his subconscious.

"Your vision might be clouded," Ashni said. Kyren hadn't been paying attention as the darkness had responded for him, but something she said drew his attention, fueling him to fight back against the darkness. It beat against him, pounding him, pushing him down, deeper and deeper,

"You're clouded by love, Kyren. By the desire to keep your family safe. By the darkness your father has planted in your mind. Let it go, Kyren! Set yourself free from his influence!" Her words resonated inside him, giving him just enough strength to wiggle out from darkness' grasp. It wasn't much, and darkness still had its hold, but he wasn't lost as he had been before.

Hours later, Jesyth approached him with a plan. Vaxon had threatened Jesyth's sister, who was dying. Kyren felt a twinge of sympathy for both of them, but darkness quickly squelched it. Jesyth wanted Kyren's help—to lead the Magi west to Komesten, instead of north. He also wanted Kyren to keep him company through telepathy as he escaped.

Kyren neither agreed nor disagreed. He was exhausted—mentally, physically, emotionally.

He just wanted all of this to end.

Mordzar wanted his help in the rebellion, Jesyth wanted him to help the Magi since he turned himself in, Eiridan had given up on him, Kanir and Cathri wanted him to do the right thing… Vaxon wanted him to die. Darkness wanted him to slaughter everything.

Everything wanted him.

He was being ripped into so many different directions, he no longer had any idea which way was up and which way was down.

"We are all family Kyren. Being a Magi is a family in and of itself. We're supposed to look out for one another," Dyrdra whispered to him. Here she was, lying on her deathbed. It took so much out of her just to speak, and she used what little strength she had to convince him to help them.

Nyk, Eiridan, and Jaeyria came to him with a plan. They all had been contacted by Vaxon, or Vassti in Jaeyria's case. They wanted to surrender to Vaxon. It was the quickest and easiest way to get inside the castle. When they took Vaxon by surprise, they could defeat him and save their families. It was a well-thought out plan, but reckless just the same. Kyren wasn't sure even with most of the Magi at their strongest if they could kill Vaxon in a fight.

It was tempting.

"Your family is a lame excuse, so don't use it," Reth told him when he came to try to convince Kyren himself.

# DARK MAGI

"A *lame... excuse?*" With darkness still warring with him internally, it wasn't hard to make Kyren furious.

"Are you really going to pity party over yourself because your daddy has your wife and kids? That's like most of the people here Kyren! That's me. We're all in the same boat. Your family is just as important as ours, but we're still going to do what's right. You can't use an excuse that we could all use but won't."

"*You shut up.* You have no idea what you're saying. I would die for them; they're not my excuse."

"Okay, let's go with the scenario that I have no idea what I'm saying. You are willing to kill and destroy anything for your father so he will let your wife live. But it's an ongoing process. Your family will never be safe until you take them from Vaxon. You can kill all of us and your father will get to rule in peace again, but do you think he'll let you and your family live somewhere? He will always hold them against you. The process will only end when they're dead, Kyren. If you take them out of his hands and take him down now, he can never use them against you again."

"I have done all I can to keep them alive. I've tried for years to free them… everything."

"And I'm not saying that you haven't. I am saying that you couldn't. You can only take down your father with the Magi by your side. And the same goes for us. We could never get freedom for us or our families by ourselves. Only you can help us with that."

Could they? All sneak in, work together as Magi to defeat Vaxon?

"Kyren," Reth said. "If you allow yourself to fall into your darkness, you will become worse than your father. He wants that, and if you keep this up, you'll allow it. Don't allow it. We're all in this together. I want my family just as much."

The words Reth spoke reached the part of Kyren that was losing his war with darkness. They gave him strength, made him want to fight, want to try.

Hours later, Nyk stormed over to Kyren, shaking. He kicked Kyren in the face, making Kyren reel from the blow. His jaw was probably broken, just like Eiridan had broken his nose. His leg still burned so he couldn't move it.

"Shara's dead. We were ambushed by a small raiding party." Nyk spoke through gritted teeth.

Kyren smirked. "Maybe you shouldn't be working for Vaxon then. Let me guess; you failed to please him?"

# DARK MAGI

Nyk brought a dagger to Kyren's throat. "Our past aside, I'll kill you, Kyren. Don't think I won't."

Kyren pressed his neck up against the blade until blood welled underneath, pooling down his neck. "Do it."

Reth snatched Nyk's hand away. "Nyk... Don't take your grief out on Kyren."

Nyk glared at Reth, but was interrupted by Kanir.

"My sister is dead because *you* refuse to help us!" Kanir shouted.

Kyren swallowed, but didn't show them any of the raging emotions battering against him. Pain, guilt, rage, hopelessness, despair, courage, a burning desire to do what was right, but the doubt and darkness inside him held him back.

"She... she..." Kanir screamed, charging for Kyren, but Reth held him back. "You *coward!* Help us! How can you sit there idle while more of us are *dying?"* Kyren didn't notice all the other Magi gathered around them in a circle.

"I told you once and I'll tell you again: all of you *will die!* His castle is a fortress with defenses many of you have *never* seen before. There is no way in! At least not quick enough to stop him. The *instant* we attack the gates, he will kill our families! Attacking his castle literally is choosing their deaths! Is that what you want?" Kyren's voice was hoarse, for he no longer had the strength to fight or resist.

"Maybe," Eiridan said, stepping forward. "If taking Vaxon down and freeing Castre from his reign means that we have to make sacrifices, then so be it."

Kyren almost laughed. Here he was, Eiridan the Healer, the one who refused to hurt others, encouraging all of them to just let their families die.

"If that's what it takes." Eriswen stepped up beside Eiridan, and her tone left no room for arguments. "You said a true bond between family means sacrificing your own soul for their sake. And I think you're right. But... What if true sacrifice means doing the *right* thing...? Even if it will get your family killed?"

Jaeyria nodded, grabbing Eiridan's hand. "Maybe that's the true meaning of sacrifice. Like what Jahad did for us."

"Or Mathas." Enya murmured it softly, and all the Magi lowered their heads at their old teacher's memory.

"You *have* to take down your father. This... Kyren, this is your chance! Your chance to overthrow him once and for all. To end all the torture he's done to you your entire life. This is your chance to have vengeance. But we can't do it without you. You have to lead the army, because they can't fight without a leader, and that's what you are. It's what you've always been. We cannot take him down without you. We need your information on his castle. Please, Kyren... Make the right choice. Don't let the darkness inside you take over. Don't let it win. Fight back. You're strong enough; I know you can do it."

Kyren wasn't sure who spoke. Perhaps it was Eiridan, the Healer who had always helped him before. Maybe it was Nyk or Reth, who had known him when he was just a young child. Or Mordzar who knew a lot of what his father had done when he was younger. Maybe it was Eriswen, the feisty shield wizard. It could have been Jaeyria, bluntly telling him the brutal truth. It could have been the air mage, or Kanir in honor of his sister's memory. Or Ashni. It could even have been Jesyth inside his thoughts, or even his dying sister.

Who spoke the words didn't matter.

What mattered was what the words did for Kyren.

They reached a part of Kyren that had slowly begun to give up in the fight with darkness. He was too exhausted to fight anymore, too broken to care.

# JOANNA WHITE

*You will become your father. That's what he wants.*

*I would rather die than see you become Vaxon.*

*We need you.*

*Kyren, I need you,* Ashyra had whispered to him.

*Kyren,* Jahad had stated, *do not allow your father's evil deeds to dishearten you.*

*You have much light inside you, Kyren. I am so proud of you. You have overcome the evil surrounding you and fought it each and every day. I know, one day, you will become a greater Magi than your father, or even me,* Mathas had told him one day.

*More powerful?* Kyren had asked.

Mathas shook his head. *Greater does not always mean more power. Let the light inside you grow and seek the Father's guidance. Let Him guide you. Then, and only then, will you become greater.*

*Kyren, I know your farther is evil. But don't allow your hatred for him to consume you,* Mathas had encouraged him, urging him to push the darkness away. *One day, it will create a void inside you that you cannot escape. Your hatred will turn you into him. Do not become your father. Be better than him.*

Could he? Be better than Vaxon?

# DARK MAGI

Could he overcome all the years of verbal abuse, physical, and mental torture that Vaxon had put him through?

Could he, with the other Magi, fight and destroy Vaxon?

Could he?

Kyren spoke words that none of them expected, words that sent shock waves pounding against each and every Magi.

"Alright, fine. Everyone listen up. If you want to attack the castle, this is how we have to do it."

**JOANNA WHITE**

# CHAPTER TEN

JAHAD WAS DEAD.

His head had been impaled on a spike and left outside the city gates. Jahad's eyes were closed, but his expression was not one of fear or horror.

It was one of pity.

Kyren swallowed back a lump in his throat and had to clench his fists to keep from calling darkness around him. More than anything, he wanted to collapse, to scream, to cry… But he couldn't.

He had taken his position as leader of the army in Jahad's place. As Prince Kyren, it was up to him to lead the rebellion. That morning, Kyren had a war meeting with the Magi and the generals of the army to discuss the plan for the siege. Besieging the city would take two weeks at the least. Even then, that was *if* luck was on their side and nothing went wrong.

# DARK MAGI

His family didn't have weeks.

They were going to have to find a way to do this quickly and efficiently. "Get in positions," Kyren ordered. Men rode on horses to carry the messages throughout the entire army. Despite the fact that Vaxon had believed all rebellion had been squelched, Jahad had managed to gather thousands of allies all across Castre. It seemed most of the people were just as tired of Vaxon's rule as the Magi were.

Jahad had been Vaxon's High General, which meant that he easily convinced over 20,000 men to defect, leaving Vaxon with 30,000 in his main army. Kyren knew that 15,000 soldiers were left inside the city, and the rest were outside of it, preparing for war.

Between the soldiers Jahad had recruited, along with the other allies, they had 25,000 soldiers total. It wasn't exactly ideal; usually sieges lasted months, and Kyren knew from his training, for a siege to be successful, double the amount of soldiers inside the city was needed. Sometimes even triple.

This wasn't going to be easy.

Then again, nothing in life ever was.

"Our plan will work." Kyren turned his head at the sound of a voice, to see Eiridan riding up beside him. Jaeyria was behind him, clutching the Healer's waist as if he was a lifeline.

Kyren averted his eyes, feeling a lump form in his throat. All he could do in reply was force a grunt. He was concentrating on the upcoming battle, and the plan, so the last thing he wanted was to be distracted with his worries and fears. Eiridan's annoying optimism and compassionate nature only reminded Kyren of what he was worried about.

His family.

He was used to isolating himself mentally, emotionally, and physically. The only attachments he had were to Ashyra, Ren, and Rya. Outside of that, he wanted no friends, but here he was; building friendships with several Magi.

*Love is weakness,* Vaxon had often told him. *A weakness your enemies will use against you.* Vaxon had often screamed the words while he was beating a young Kyren. As Kyren had grown, Vaxon had proved the words true time and time again. Anything Kyren would attach himself to emotionally—from animals and pets to people—Vaxon would destroy, kill, and rip away from him.

*Love is weakness.*

Now… Kyren had more to lose than he was comfortable with.

# DARK MAGI

They *all* did.

Kyren glanced from Eiridan and Jaeyria to Mordzar, who rode a horse on the other side. The man had known Kyren as a child but they had parted ways as they had grown older and the Metal Mage had been working more closely with the army due to his nobleman family. He trusted the man, especially when it came to matters of war. "Mordzar," Kyren addressed. "While Eiridan, Jaeyria and Nyk are sneaking inside under the pretense of surrender, you and Eriswen lead the siege on the south wall. It's closest to the castle, so it's just as heavily fortified as the northern gates."

At his instructions, Mordzar nodded his head. "I have several of my father's old allies accompanying the regiment. Shall I take them with us?" Mordzar's father, as one of the leading nobles in the rebellion against Vaxon, would have more allies than anyone else they knew.

Kyren nodded in response.

"General!" At the sound of a messenger's voice, Kyren shifted his gaze to see a rider heading their way. All the messengers had been instructed to call Kyren "General." He covered his face and only spoke to those he needed: the Magi, messengers, and the real generals of the army. Vaxon had many spies, so he had to keep his presence a secret as long as possible.

His wife and children's lives depended on it.

"What is it?" Kyren deepened his voice. With his current mood, it wasn't hard.

"Zentra and Yuknao have fled."

Kyren cursed. Jesyth had left early that morning; Kyren understood, since his sister Dyrdra was dying, but it still lessened their numbers. With the army not having enough numbers for a siege, they needed every available Magi possible. Now two more had left.

That left thirteen.

At the sound of a horn blowing from inside Komesten's walls, Kyren nodded to Eiridan and Jaeyria. "Go."

Nyk, who was riding a stallion on their other side, gave Kyren a curt nod before trailing after them.

"Enya, Evon, and Ashni, I want you at the western wall. It's less fortified, so you might have a better chance to break through their walls and get inside the city. Once there, just continue pushing their troops back until we can break through the northern gates."

The three Magi all nodded before riding off with another regiment. "What do you want me to do?" Boli, the young Water

# DARK MAGI

Magi, looked up at Kyren. Despite their situation, there was no fear in the young man's eyes; only determination. Kyren felt a twinge of pity toward such a young child who had grown up much too quickly.

"Stay with Dyrdra," Kyren replied. "I promised Jesyth I'd take care of her, but I can't while I'm fighting. Go back to the med-camp and stay with her. Okay?"

The young man nodded and spurred his horse to a gallop.

"Who's attacking the east wall?" Lyva glanced up at him from her spot on the ground.

"You and Kanir."

Kanir met his eyes and then nodded. "Alright. Let's go, Lyva." Kanir's mare galloped away, with Lyva's wolf-form not too far behind. They had both just lost a sibling, reminding Kyren of the memory he'd relived the previous day. *Korrah. Kassan.* He brushed it off and forced himself to focus on the task at hand.

"What do we do?" Reth smirked at him from his spot on the ground.

Kyren dismounted and smacked his horse to send it away. "Fight, of course." Even though it had been a rhetorical question, Kyren replied anyway.

"Um, since you're the general, shouldn't you... I don't know, maybe stay on your horse where your men can find you?" Reth lifted an eyebrow, twirling a sword in his right hand.

Kyren glared at him, unsheathing his own sword. "You just want me out of the way, so you can get more kills."

Reth grinned. "Yep, that's about it."

Kyren raised his sword and glared at Vaxon's army charging toward them. "Not a chance. Ready, Reth?"

Reth punched his right fist into his left palm. "I'm always ready."

At his friend's old phrase, Kyren rolled his eyes, but the two darted into the heart of the fray together.

Most of Vaxon's army lined up outside the city gates and met theirs in the middle of a wide field perfectly fit for battle. Kyren and Reth wholeheartedly jumped at the opportunity to be on the front lines, fighting toe-to-toe with their enemies.

The first line of Vaxon's forces were spearmen on horses. Distantly, Kyren knew a smarter man would have stayed on his horse, but being in the heat of a battle once again reminded him so much of the old days. He couldn't help but dance with death, teasing and testing it repetitively.

Fighting in battle was the only thing, outside of being with Ashyra, that made him forget his pain.

# DARK MAGI

Having to refrain from using his darkness to keep Vaxon from sensing him was probably the best thing that could have happened to him. It enabled him to enjoy battle without worrying about the darkness taking him over again.

Instead, he used an Elogii blade, made from *Elogiian* crystal, perfect for a Magi to wield. The blade glowed a bright blue, which contrasted with the silver hue that the moon emitted.

Using the magical energy from his blade to increase his strength, he jumped as high as he could. He landed smoothly behind one soldier on a horse, stabbed him in the back, and then shoved him off. With smooth grace, he snatched the reins in his left hand, as he wielded his sword in his right. At the same time that he turned the horse to the left, he sliced the man on his right.

A rider on his left jabbed a spear toward his chest. Kyren twisted to the right, ducking to the side of his horse while holding onto the reins tight enough to keep from falling. Jerking the reins to the right as hard as he could, he waited for his horse to shift positions. When it did, he slipped his blade inside the man's spear to break through his defense and stab his side, in his armor's weak point.

# JOANNA WHITE

Kyren dove off the horse onto the ground in a forward roll. As he rose to his feet, another soldier rode straight for him, driving his spear toward Kyren's chest, slicing through his leather armor.

He preferred leather for maneuverability, but the drawbacks were that it didn't hold up against most weapons. Then again, typically, Kyren had his magic and didn't worry too much about stopping weapons from getting too close.

Kyren cursed and attacked as high up as he could, but the man blocked with the middle of his spear. He pressed against Kyren's sword, causing Kyren to lose his balance. With a wicked grin, Kyren sliced his sword across the man's saddle. It surprised him, and he laughed, thinking Kyren had missed him.

Just as the man jabbed his spear toward Kyren again, his saddle came unhitched and he fell to the ground. The horse had no time to stop, however, and trampled him. The sound of bones crunching couldn't be heard over the sounds of the battle raging around them. Men were yelling and screaming, some in pain, some with furious war cries. Metal clanged against metal and the smell of blood was in the air.

# DARK MAGI

Reth had been fighting soldiers to Kyren's left. "General, you're fighting on the wrong side!"

Kyren rolled his eyes, ducking underneath another spear, before stabbing another soldier in the side as he rode passed. "I'm right where I want to be! It's easier to kill more men than you from here."

Reth glared at him for a second, before making a show out of head-butting one soldier, stabbing him in the foot, then decapitating him. He drew runes into the air, which flashed before his armor changed. Elven armor glittered gold, making it look like liquid in the night sky. Wings sprouted from his back, lightweight and yet strong enough to lift him into the air. A bow appeared from his hands as he took flight, hovering above Vaxon's army. With that, he grinned and fired arrow after arrow, killing man after man. "Twelve! That makes twelve! How many do you have?"

Kyren cursed, choosing to ignore Reth's sarcastic question. "I hate warrior magic," he muttered.

Glancing around the battlefield, he spotted just what he needed:

A giant dramon.

Kyren grabbed a wandering horse whose rider had died and hopped on. He spurred the horse and galloped to his right, where the giants were charging from Vaxon's army into theirs. As his horse bolted through the field, he swung his sword left-and-right, killing as many men as he could.

The legends of the dramon were that they were once giants who had been cursed long ago. *"They starve to death and yet never die,"* Korrah had whispered to him one night.

*"Stop it! You're just trying to scare me!"* Kyren complained.

*Kassan laughed. "You scared, brother?"*

*Kyren pouted. "No! Of course I'm not scared!"*

*"Go to bed, you two! If you don't, the giant dramon will smash through the walls and eat you for a late night snack!" Korrah had tickled them both.*

Kyren shook off the memory and pulled his horse to a stop as he neared the creature. It was nearly fifty foot tall, with gray skin that was wilted and peeling off. A few of its bones were visible, covered by patches of skin here and there. Its beard and hair still barely clung to its dirty face. It swiped its hand across the field, slaughtering men by the dozens.

Seeing a mammoth pulling one of the catapults toward the city walls, Kyren grinned, jumped off his horse, and darted that direction. *This is incredibly stupid,* Kyren thought. With that, he clambered over the side of the catapult until he thought he was high enough.

Then he jumped from the catapult onto the top of the forty-foot-tall mammoth. The war machine was close enough to the wall, so he nodded to several soldiers, who cut the mammoth lose. He grasped the ropes controlling the mammoth, and then charged straight for the giant dramon.

The mammoth plowed into the dramon, who hadn't expected it. *Good thing dramon are stupid.* The two clashed, and fell onto the ground. The earth trembled and dust stirred up everywhere, making his eyes water. He tumbled over and over again, not knowing which direction was up or down.

When he shook his head to orientate himself, he noticed one of the mammoth's tusks had pierced the dramon.

Reth, who had banked over that way to see what the commotion was, glared at him. "Whatever! Not nearly as epic as some of my moves!"

Kyren smirked. "That makes eighteen." He unsheathed his blade and darted back into the heat of battle.

# JOANNA WHITE

## CHAPTER ELEVEN

ALREADY, THEY HAD been fighting for nearly six hours. Kyren and Reth had stopped briefly for a short break, before jumping right back into the fighting. *Nsai* crawlers had been brought to drain the acid from the moat, using their radioactive suction claws, and after several hours of holding off Vaxon's field army, the acid was finally all gone. The mammoths all plowed forward, carrying a battering ram that they pounded against the front gates again and again.

It was finally starting to crack.

At the same time that was going on, catapults rained boulders toward the inside of the city. Flaming arrows flew from both sides, piercing men's armor and lighting them on fire. Goblins and ogres darted from Vaxon's army, clashing against brownies and gnomes from their allies. Phoenixes,

# DARK MAGI

griffins, and dragons flew, furiously fighting each other on both sides. Giant ladders were brought up against the walls, and as men tried to climb, archers at the top took them down, preventing their army from reaching the top of the city walls.

*Kyren.* The voice in his mind came from Jesyth, who had figured out how to use telepathy to communicate. *You need to get here, now!*

He couldn't use any of his magic to pry into Jesyth's mind to see what the situation was and there wasn't any time. Darting over to where Reth was sipping a drink of water, he clenched his fists. "We need to get into the castle. Something's gone wrong."

Reth paled for a moment, and Kyren knew they were both thinking of their wives and children. He nodded and followed after Kyren. "What's the situation around the city?"

Kyren replied as they made their way through their side of the battlefield, where the fighting was thinnest. "Yuknao is dead. Lyva and Kanir broke through the east wall two hours ago. Half an hour ago I received word that Enya, Evon, and Ashni broke through the west wall, so the regiments from the west and east are both pushing toward the center. Mordzar and Eris are having as much trouble as we are."

Reth nodded. "Well, if we're sneaking into the castle, does that mean you and I are going to take on Vaxon?"

Kyren paused, deep in thought. "No. No, to take him down, we're going to need *all* the Magi. All of the rest of us, working together."

Much to Kyren's surprise, it only took half an hour to send word to everyone. They all traveled to the east wall—which was closest—to get inside Komesten. The streets were all deserted of people, but full of soldiers. Most were frantic, desperately trying to push back the rebels from the west and east walls, while still holding back those besieging the north and south. Kyren led the Magi through the back streets to avoid the soldiers, and as they grew closer to the castle, the Nires castle guards.

Ten minutes later, they were standing in front of the castle moat. Acid glowed brightly, adding color to the gray-hue of night. It bubbled and gurgled, making all the Magi nervous.

"I thought you said acid only surrounded the *city* walls," Eriswen pointed out.

"I thought you said acid only surrounded the castle walls." Ashni

# DARK MAGI

scratched her head, as all the Magi looked to Kyren for an explanation.

"It surrounds both." Kyren shrugged.

"How are we supposed to get over this?" Ashni asked.

"What about the creatures that ate the acid around the city walls?" Mordzar crossed his arms.

Kyren shook his head. "It would attract way too much attention."

"Can't you teleport us?" Kanir glanced at him.

Kyren shook his head. "Not with Vaxon so close. He'll be able to sense my magic." After pausing, he continued. "Eriswen, Mordzar, can you work together to create a bridge made out of your shields and metal?"

"After all the fighting, I don't know if I have enough energy to keep it up long enough for everyone to cross." Eriswen sighed.

"Do a fusion of magic energy. It will make you both stronger, and cost less energy since you're sharing the load."

Their eyes widened. "It's possible to do that? Mathas never mentioned it!" Mordzar exclaimed.

"It's a difficult technique to master, but we don't have months. We have minutes, so hurry."

Both nodded, clasped hands and closed eyes.

Blue Mathanos highlighted their skin as Eriswen's transparent shields flickered to life. It hurled across the moat, soon reinforced by Mordzar's metal. The newly formed metal and energy bridge was outlined in bright blue Mathanos. For a moment, it disappeared and Eriswen's brow furrowed with her face covered in sweat. Mordzar clung tightly to her and it looked as if the two held each other upright.

Finally, their makeshift bridge appeared and this time it stayed.

"Go, now!" Mordzar called to them.

Kyren pressed a foot down onto it, testing the weight. When it stayed, he and the other Magi hurried across as quickly as they could, followed closely by Eris and Mordzar.

They were nearly there. Acid bubbled up on either side of them. Just as Kyren reached the other side, Eris and Mordzar ran to the middle of the bridge. Eriswen nearly collapsed from exhaustion, but Mordzar caught her, despite how tired he looked.

Mordzar shoved her forward and the two made it across.

Kyren looked at Enya, and then at the castle wall in front of them.

# DARK MAGI

She nodded without even having to be asked. It only took seconds for the air around them to stir. It whirled and blew around them furiously, lifting them all into the air and over the wall. Before she could collapse, Kyren caught her and held her upright.

"What about the war hounds?" Evon asked.

"During a siege, they're locked up. Our best way in is through the barracks. Come on." Kyren helped an exhausted Enya, as Mordzar and Eriswen helped each other down the nearby stair way.

"Evon, Kanir, Reth. We have to take out the guards in here as quickly and quietly as possible. There's no time to waste; we can't let them raise the alarm." The three men nodded and led the way beside Kyren. He turned to Mordzar, Eriswen, and Enya. "Don't use any magic in here. Take the time to regenerate it before we reach the throne room." They nodded as Kyren stepped up beside the three men.

Kyren shoved open the barrack doors and Mordzar closed it as quietly as possible once the Magi were inside.

Kyren darted forward, stabbing one guard in the neck as he covered his mouth to muffle the screams. Evon formed a wave of water, which took out four more who had charged in their direction. Reth zipped around the room after having used some sort of armor that increased his speed. Kanir didn't bother to use his lightning, which was too loud. Apparently, he had decided to use an Elogii blade similar to Kyren's.

Soon, all the guards in the barracks were dead.

"We make a pretty good team," Evon said.

Kanir shook his head. "Surprisingly."

Reth grinned. "That brings me up to five-hundred -forty-two kills."

Kyren stomped on the head of one guard who was still stirring. "Five-hundred-forty-*five.*"

"Enough with counting kills, you two. Let's move," Mordzar said, stepping forward with Eriswen next to him. "I knew we shouldn't have let you two fight together."

"I'm surprised you don't remember what a great team we make," Kyren muttered.

"I grew up in this palace, too, so of course I remember the trouble you two always got yourselves in!" Mordzar glared at Reth and Kyren, but it was lighthearted.

"Yeah, that's great, but we have a mission, guys!" Eriswen hissed.

**184**

# DARK MAGI

Kyren shoved himself against a wall in the back corner of the room, revealing a secret passageway. "This way." Fortunately, Reth was able to switch into armor that glowed bright enough to light the way. Even if Reth hadn't, Kyren would have known it by heart. He had traveled it many times, and with each step, memories surfaced. Gritting his teeth, he pulled up his walls around his mind, mentally blocking out his mother. The air was damp and stale, and water trickled down the stones, making *drip-drip-drip* sounds that gave Kyren the shivers.

Before he opened the door that led out, he stopped them all. "Once we open this door, the Nires will be waiting."

"Any ideas how to take them out?" Ashni questioned.

"Yeah. I've got an idea." Kyren looked at Reth, wagging his eyebrows. "We're going to have to do a mercenary."

Reth groaned. "No. No. No. *Not a mercenary!*"

"*Do* a mercenary?" Ashni raised an eyebrow.

"Just do what I tell you to do."

JOANNA WHITE

# CHAPTER TWELVE

KYREN STOOD BEFORE the Nires with the Magi behind him, locked in dark chains he had used his magic to create. Reth knew the plan well, and he played the part, cursing Kyren and struggling against the chains, but to no avail.

Kyren had clouded all of their minds, protecting them from Vassti's prying powers to keep their plan from failing before it started. His energy was dwindling by the second, so they had to hurry.

The Nires saw him and opened the way into the throne room.

Inside, the situation was worse than Kyren could have imagined. Eiridan was on the floor, paler than a ghost, and it didn't look like he was breathing.

As soon as Kyren saw his friend, he jerked forward, but the Nires on either side of him prevented him.

# DARK MAGI

"Oh, don't worry." Vaxon nudged Eiridan with his foot and his gaze shot up to meet his son's. "Your weakling of a friend *might* survive. After all, I just cast Consumption on him."

Kyren gasped at the name of the spell. He had cast the spell before, but never the way that Vaxon did. Vaxon was one of the most powerful Dark Mages in existence. If his father had cast it, then it meant almost certain death for Eiridan.

Immediately focusing to his task, Kyren threw darkness away from his body, yelling the spell out loud to add extra energy to it. *"Void!"*

His energy was as dark as a starless sky as it formed a circle around Vaxon. Kyren heard Vaxon's laugh over the noise, before the circle itself was consumed. *"Dissipate!"* Vaxon shouted in reply.

Kyren gasped. Even he had no idea that his father could nullify his darkness like that, but it took its toll on the king; sweat beaded on Vaxon's brow. Despite it, Vaxon threw darkness around Kyren to keep him from moving.

Kyren struggled against it, shoving it backward, but nothing he did worked. Panic settled in, but he tried calming his mind and thoughts. *There's still the back-up plan.* He hoped for the best. His heart sank; their second plan didn't come without sacrifices.

That was when he saw all the people in the room, each one surrounded by Nires. One woman was on the floor, her throat ripped out. Despite the state her body was in, something about her eyes reminded him of Eiridan.

"Mother." Mordzar stared at a woman to the far right, standing beside a man Kyren easily recognized as one of the nobles, Mordzar's father, Lord Malthus. Behind them cowered their young daughter, Myra.

Vaxon's darkness seethed against Kyren's flesh, freezing his bones.

They were all paralyzed.

Every single one of the Magi's family members were here, bound and helpless before them. The full force of the horror they faced struck him. Vaxon would kill them all and force the Magi to watch, unable to save their families.

Vaxon's eyes met Mordzar's. He nodded his head, and on his command, a Nires sliced Lord Malthus' throat, followed by his wife. Mordzar screamed but it did little good. His parents' bodies fell to the ground, unmoving. Blood pooled underneath them, staining the white marble bright crimson. Myra was yanked forward and thrown at Mordzar's feet.

"Will you join me?" Vaxon stepped forward so that he was just behind Mordzar's sister.

"It's okay, big brother. I understand." Myra kept her gaze firmly on her brother.

Tears glistened in Mordzar's eyes as he whispered back to her. "No," he said, his voice rising stronger. "No. I will never join you!"

Vaxon nodded. "Very well." He opened his hand and tendrils of darkness snaked from them, choking Myra. Her face reddened and her body twitched and jerked, but Mordzar struggled against Vaxon's magic.

Finally, her tiny body lay still. All Mordzar could do was close his eyes and let the tears fall. Kyren sucked in a deep breath.

Vaxon stepped to the next person in line—Eris.

Eriswen groaned as one Nires held a small dragon youngling by the tail.

"And you?" At the wave of Vaxon's hand, the Nires holding the dragon youngling marched forward. The Nires held a claw to the dragon's throat, who yowled in response.

Eris hesitated.

"Eris, don't do it!" Mordzar yelled.

Eris slowly nodded, as tears fell from her face. "Yes. I'll join you. I can't let Ionaen's last hatchling die."

Vaxon smiled. "Then give me your Blood Oath of Servitude." He waved his hand, releasing only Eris' hands. She sliced her palm and recited the Blood Oath.

"*No!*" Mordzar screamed, but it was no use. All the Magi looked defeated at seeing one of their own by Vaxon's side. He gestured to the dais and instructed her to stand there. For the first time Kyren noticed Zentra and Jaeyria.

"They betrayed us?" Mordzar glanced at Kyren.

Kyren ground his teeth, glaring at Jaeyria. He shifted his gaze to Eiridan. "How could you have betrayed him like that, Jaeyria? He loved you!"

"I did this to save him!" she cried.

Kyren cursed at her with a snarl. *I can't let any more people die, or any more of them turn.* With newfound strength, Kyren called darkness to his mind, and began pulling Mathanos to his body. For the spell he was going to do, he needed all the energy he could get.

"I surrender." As Kanir recited the Blood Oath and stepped toward Vaxon, Kyren's stomach twisted. One by one, the

# DARK MAGI

Magi were either turning to Vaxon's side, or their families were dying.

There was nothing he could do. He prayed to the Father he could cast the spell in time and that the other half of the plan would work. Kanir took his place beside Zentra, Eriswen, and Jaeyria on the dais.

Vassti strolled into the room, accompanied by Nyk.

Reth gritted his teeth, but made no other movements.

"Traitor," Reth hissed beneath his breath venomously. How could it have come to this? Kyren's friends losing everyone they loved, Magi turning against Magi, brother betraying brother? "How could you do this to me? To Ika and Idan?" Reth shouted toward his brother.

Nyk stood beside the other traitorous Magi, refusing to even look in his brother's direction.

One by one, Vaxon made the Magi an offer. Two siblings, Ashni and Evon, offended Vaxon, so he stabbed them both and Kyren's stomach twisted. Another Magi named Enya chose to surrender to Vaxon.

He couldn't blame either side; the Magi being angry at the traitors or the Magi choosing to surrender. Where were Ashyra, Ren, and Rya? Had Vaxon already killed them? The thought paralyzed him internally with fear, but he realized that they were still alive. If Vaxon was going to kill them, he would do it in front of Kyren to watch his son suffer the most. Tears burned in Kyren's eyes.

What would he do, when Ashyra and his children were brought in front of him? Would he stay strong, choose to die, knowing it would end in their deaths? Could he stand with his friends who chose not to surrender or would he stand over by Nyk and the traitors?

Kyren closed his eyes, frantically calling more and more energy to his body. He felt trapped and helpless... imprisoned by his father's darkness once again with no way of escape.

A door to the side opened, revealing Jesyth. He walked stiffly up onto the dais, taking a place beside Nyk. Both of them stood behind Vassti, as the other traitors—Zentra, Jaeyria, Kanir, and Eriswen—lined up on their other side. Two Nires stormed in the room, one clutching Dyrdra, the other clutching Boli.

Kyren's heart sank. He had failed to keep his promise to Jesyth to keep his sister safe.

"Jesyth, because you have surrendered to me, your sister Dyrdra will live, along with her friend. Here is your proof. Take her to the dungeons. Along with that foolish boy," Vaxon drawled, as if he was bored.

Boli fought to free himself, but as the Nires yanked him away, his gaze met Dyrdra's helpless one. Dyrdra called out for Jesyth, who remained stoic.

Vaxon smiled and then his eyes met Kyren's, as he gestured to Jesyth. "Did you know this is your brother?"

It was as if all the air in the room had been sucked away.

Kyren gritted his teeth, his concentration temporarily broken, but kept his face impassive. "It's not surprising, with how much you sleep around. What is this, my second half brother discovered in not even a week?"

Vaxon's jaw clenched for a moment and his eyes narrowed. "I will get to you later, *Kyren.*" Again, he waved his hand.

Reth tensed beside him. His wife, Ika, thrashed as two Nires shoved her forward. "Reth!"

"Ika!" Beside her shrank a young boy, Idan.

The Nires grasped Ika's arms and brought her forward in front of Reth. Idan was thrown down beside them.

Pain flared in Reth's gaze and he struggled against the spell keeping him paralyzed. Kyren shifted more energy inside himself, hoping to gain enough to cast the spell before they all ran out of time, before any more of his friends had to die.

Before his wife and children had to die.

"What of you, Redblade? Shall I start with your lovely wife, or perhaps begin crushing your young son's skull?"

Reth glared in Vaxon with a defiant gaze. "I'll *kill you, you piece of scum!*"

Vaxon threw a dark spear through Ika's stomach. Her eyes widened for a second, before her body collapsed. Blood flowed, as it had so many times that night, pooling underneath her body, staining Reth's shoes.

*He's making her die slowly so Reth will have to watch.* Anger coursed through Kyren's veins.

"Ika! Ika, it's okay. I'm—I'm here." Kyren could hear how desperately Reth tried to keep it together as his wife died right before his eyes.

"Do you surrender, or will you watch your son die too?" Vaxon demanded.

Reth's gaze flashed briefly to Kyren, who nodded once, as if reassuring him. *Go ahead. Do what you have to do to keep him alive. I understand,* Kyren wanted to say. He would do the same to save his family.

# DARK MAGI

*Ashyra. Ren. Rya.* Their names brought pain and terror to his chest, made his heart race, his fists wanted to clench and unclench but he couldn't move, which only fueled his panic and frustration.

With hunched shoulders, Reth bowed his head. "I surrender."

What few Magi were left gasped in utter shock.

Kyren froze, and forced himself not to listen as Reth recited the Blood Oath. He didn't want to look as Reth took his place beside his brother Nyk at Vaxon's side.

Kyren felt nothing as Vaxon stood in front of him.

Doors slammed open and Ashyra, Rya, and Ren were dragged out. Ashyra cried out for Kyren, but the Nires on either side of her held her back.

He struggled against his father's darkness, desperately trying to reach her. "It's okay, Ashyra. We're going to be okay..." Kyren murmured, much like Reth had a few minutes earlier. Closing his eyes, he finally finished calling darkness inside him. *"Release!"* A cloud of Kyren's dark energy whirled between him and Vaxon, shoving against Vaxon's darkness. It freed him and he charged forward, but Vaxon waved his hands and his own dark energy pierced Kyren's.

Kyren's spell disappeared.

How… how was Vaxon this powerful?

Kyren lunged toward Ashyra, but four Nires charged toward him. He kicked one in the chest and elbowed another. The last two tackled him to the ground and painfully wrenched him to his feet, jerking his arms behind his back. He didn't feel the pain from the slash marks as their claws tore his skin. No, Kyren felt nothing, saw nothing except his wife and children.

"My—my family will *never* let you get away with this, Vaxon!" Ashyra screamed at the top of her lungs. She trashed and struggled against the Nires, fighting to reach their precious children. "My family will bring war upon you!"

Vaxon threw his head back and *laughed.* "Then let there be war!"

Ashyra stopped struggling and Kyren's heart sank.

Two more Nires dropped her at Kyren's feet. Though she was crying and sobbing, she smiled at him, lighting up his entire world. "*I see you,*" she whispered. It brought back so many memories, bringing warmth and comfort into his heart. It was their phrase. It expressed how deeply they loved each other and how she saw the real him deep inside. It was their loyalty and utter devotion to each other; everything.

"I see you." His reply was a slight shift in the air currents.

Her gaze held his as Vaxon slammed his hand into her chest.

Tears spilled out of Kyren's eyes like a furious and wild hurricane, but he couldn't look away as Vaxon ripped out her heart.

Vaxon shoved his hands in Kyren's face so that her blood was pressed against his skin. Kyren's stomach lurched as he gagged and turned away, throwing up onto the floor below him. He struggled in the Nires' hold on him, but the agony he felt weakened him.

One Nires grabbed each of his son's limbs. *"Papa! Papa! Help me! Help me!"* He shrieked, an inhuman, animalistic sound which etched itself on Kyren's soul.

Then the Nires tore him apart, limb from limb.

Kyren had no words for the sight before him. There was so much blood; there was no way to even tell the floor had ever been white marble.

*"Enough!"* Vassti screamed and her eyes flashed white. Reth burst into movement, and Kyren's heart fluttered in brief, silent relief and confused pain. Reth and Jesyth had obviously not been able to

convince Vassti to side with them against Vaxon. Only Kyren's family being brutally murdered had changed her mind. Anger gripped him but the grief weighed too heavily upon him to keep it there.

So many people had been slaughtered here, but Kyren tried to be thankful that their plan could still work now even if it came too late and at far too high a price. Without it, they wouldn't have a chance to defeat Vaxon at all.

Love was sacrifice.

*"It's what the Father did for us,"* *Vassti had whispered to him as a little boy.*

Vassti's distraction of Vaxon gave Kyren enough time to call darkness around him and teleport to the other side of the room. He grabbed a dagger from a fallen soldier, stabbed the Nires holding his infant daughter in the neck, and snatched her away. Despite the wound, the Nires stalked toward him, but he teleported to the other side of the room before the Nires could attack them.

Mordzar, Reth, and Jesyth teamed up together, temporarily holding off Vaxon. Vassti stood near Kanir, Nyk, Jaeyria, Eriswen, Zentra, and Lyva, breaking their Blood Oaths. Lyva's eyes flashed white and she blinked and was the first to snap out of the Blood Oath.

# DARK MAGI

Kyren sprinted over to her, and then teleported her to a hidden room. "Lyva… Take care of Rya… *Please*. She's all I have left. Lock the door, and… don't—don't die. Don't let my baby girl die." At the last word, Kyren choked.

Lyva nodded and smiled at him. "I won't let anything happen to her, Kyren. Go!"

He took one last glance at his daughter and returned to the throne room.

Mordzar and Jesyth struggled against Vaxon's Cyclone of Darkness.

Kyren looked around for his mother; she should have freed Nyk by then. She leaned against the wall beside the dais, clutching her stomach.

Jaeyria and Enya fought each other in a furious battle of wind and shadows, while Reth and Nyk battled furiously, brother against brother.

Kyren cursed. *She only freed a few Magi from the Blood Oaths. Vaxon must have distracted them and stabbed her.*

He had no time to help her.

Vaxon's darkness exploded toward Mordzar and Jesyth, throwing them to the other side of the room.

Kyren drew dark tendrils to his hands and snaked them at Vaxon. "You and

I have unfinished business." Hate blackened Kyren's heart.

Vaxon grinned.

Kyren's only hope was that Vaxon couldn't dispel his magic. Ashyra and Ren had died in agony because of this sadistic, twisted psychopath. The hatred inside him fueled Kyren's darkness and all he wanted was to make Vaxon suffer for all he had done. For all the Magi he had slaughtered, for Kyren's wife and son. His pain merged with his deep-rooted hatred that helped his own darkness consume him.

Vaxon rotated his hands, calling dark fire to his hands. "Dark Elements!"

Kyren cursed. It had been a spell he had never been able to master, simply because it required being one with the elements, as well as with one's own inner darkness. He was too wild and his emotions were too unstable to do it.

Dark fire flickered as the flames licked Vaxon's hands. Dark water joined it, flowing in fluid and elegant movements. Dark air formed around them, whirling and whipping Kyren's hair furiously. The earth underneath him trembled and shook, until a wall of blackened and deadened earth appeared in front of Vaxon. With a furious cry, Vaxon hurled everything he had at Kyren.

# DARK MAGI

Kyren jumped to the right, but the elements changed directions. Cursing, he threw up his hands and yelled, "Dark shield!"

The shield heated up as the dark fire licked and burned it. Dark water and air pushed against it, leaving a crack in the center. The crack spread out like spider webs when the earth pounded against it, until the shield itself shattered, hurting him as if it was part of his body. The wall slammed into him, throwing him back. He coughed and wheezed, trying to gulp air into his lungs.

"You foolish boy," Vaxon sneered as he strolled over to Kyren as he struggled to his knees. "You cannot even last a minute against my power! Mathas taught you nothing!"

Kryen saw the world in shades of black and his hands shook with the need to destroy. *Vaxon. He killed Mathas! He murdered Jahad. He ripped out Ashyra's heart, and tore Ren to pieces!* Agony swelled in his chest, so much that he couldn't breathe. He swallowed back bile, grinding his teeth together to keep from throwing up. Kyren's mind had been pried apart by Vaxon's torture, by the images haunting and plaguing him. His chest seized furiously, and his very soul had been shattered into tiny shards, like a broken mirror. One by one, Kyren's hatred shaped each fragment into weapons and sent them back along Vaxon's mental connection to him.

Kyren's darkness exploded in Vaxon's mind, grasping anything it could reach.

Vaxon stumbled backward. He had been had been arrogant and left himself mentally vulnerable, if only for a moment.

Kyren surged to his feet with Mathas' strength and energy inside him. Ashyra's hope and smile keeping him going. Ren's bold and adventurous nature, bringing him joy. Jahad's courage and compassion, pushing away the darkness. And the Father... The Father's forgiveness and even His light, as well. All of them lent him power, the power he needed to defeat Vaxon.

He lifted his hands up, throwing physical darkness at Vaxon like a hurricane, as his mental darkness still attacked Vaxon's consciousness. In desperation, Vaxon used his darkness to build back up his walls to protect his mind, but that took too much concentration.

It left him open for a physical attack.

*"Complete Consumption!"* Kyren screamed. His darkness wrapped around

# DARK MAGI

Vaxon like a cocoon. He could feel Vaxon's life force, his magic energy, his consciousness, even his soul, being drawn into Kyren.

But unlike Consumption, the caster of Complete Consumption would die.

"Father! Kyren!" a high-pitched voice squealed.

Kyren turned to see Nassia darting in the room.

Vassti saw her and screamed.

After Korah's death Vassti and even Vaxon spoiled Nassia, ironically trying to protect her from the evil in the palace.

She was a compete brat, but he'd seen too much death. He *refused* to lose anyone else.

Vaxon grinned, twisting his expression into a snarl.

Kyren's eyes widened as he shouted over the noise of the spell. "What are you doing?" His voice was barely audible over the gust spiraling around them. *He can't cast anything while fighting against Complete Consumption!*

"Nassia, leave! *Now!*" Vassti tried to stand but her words ended wet and raspy and she slumped back against the wall.

"M—Mother?" Tears brimmed in Nassia's eyes as she ran help her mother, then stared at the blood on her hands.

Vaxon's grin widened.

Kyren pressed his darkness tighter against Vaxon, hoping to stop whatever he was going to do. *"Father, don't!"*

"Eclipse."

Shadows of the past haunted Kyren, but this time his sister was the helpless one. It was the same scenario. Only this time the spell wasn't aimed at Kyren. No, this time Eclipse was aimed at Kyren's last living sibling—Nassia.

Darkness exploded from the sky, causing the ceiling to crumble. As dust and debris rained down on them all, darkness shot out toward Nassia. She stared in confusion and horror, unable to move.

Kyren cut off Complete Consumption, ignoring the agony it caused. His magical energy was completely gone. He'd cast a spell which should have killed him, then dispelled it. It was too much…he couldn't move.

Yet he did.

He darted toward Nassia and dove on top of her, calling forth a dark shield to wrap around them.

Vaxon's darkness shoved against his shield, cracking it ever-so-slowly. Kyren grunted, struggling against pain and exhaustion, desperately trying to stay awake. "Brother, here!" Nassia grabbed his wrist to

# DARK MAGI

lend him extra Mathanos. He increased the strength of the shield, desperately trying to hold up against the darkness pulsing and pushing against it.

Blackness over took his flickering vision, and unconsciousness called out to him. He was cold, oh so terribly cold. It was as if he was lost and wandering, unable to find his way back.

One by one, he saw the faces of his loved ones before his eyes, both dead and alive. Korrah and Kassan, laughing and giggling as they all played together. Mathas training with them, showing them how to use their magic for good, teaching them the ways of the Father, of His love and sacrifice. Mathas' execution, and then the Magi being hunted down. Kyren killing Kassan and then Korrah protecting Kyren. Vassti's sorrowful eyes as she looked at her last living child. Vaxon's furious training, pushing Kyren to the brink of death. Vassti's joy when she had Nassia, a new child and a fresh start from the tragedy of the past. Kyren being locked inside the prison, the countless hours of torture. Jahad being there for him, getting him through it all. Years later, as he became a slave, he saw Ashyra, her eyes... her smile. Jahad smiling warmly at them both as they said, "I do." Kyren looking into Ren's eyes for the first time, and how nervous he was at being a father, especially when it was supposed to be secret. Ren's first words, "Papa!" Ashyra and Kyren laughing, and then deciding to have a second child. The absolute love and adoration when Kyren laid eyes on his precious baby girl. Through the blood that consumed his world, Kyren focused on Ashyra's beautiful eyes. They were full of love and hope…. And peace.

*Love is weakness.*

He had loved, but it hadn't made him weak. No, it was his love for them and their love for him that pushed away his darkness. It was love that kept him from becoming his father. But…

It had also destroyed him.

Blackness swirled as it gradually formed shapes in his vision. Silhouettes darted around him, flickered, and became blurs. Color came into the world, draining away the blackness. The blurs trembled and shook, and then merged into one image.

Nassia knelt over him, crying and shaking him. His entire body was numb, and he couldn't move. Distantly, he knew that wasn't a good thing. Vassti had crawled over to him, and was clutching his hand tightly, squeezing it.

"Kyren, come back to me!" Sobs wracked her body, and Kyren was shocked to see his emotionless, impassive mother in

# DARK MAGI

such a state. "I'm so sorry, Kyren! I—I should have made things right with you sooner!" She coughed up blood and it dribbling down her chin and onto Kyren's chest.

"It's—" he choked, unable to say anymore.

"I—I love you." Vassti coughed again, and collapsed onto his chest. She breathed once, and then stopped.

Sorrow and death were constant companions that accompanied Kyren wherever he went, weighing him down, crushing his already broken body.

"M—Mother? Why did—I—Why did Father hurt you, Kyren? Why… Why is Mother not waking up?" Nassia's tears spilled onto Kyren like a flood.

*Because this is what death is. This is what Vaxon is. You never knew. We'd protected you to keep you innocent,* Kyren thought, unable to say the words out loud. They had turned her into a selfish brat but had it really been her fault? Had it truly protected her?

Mordzar, Jesyth, and Kanir were desperately tried to make it to their feet. Jaeyria stood in front of Eiridan, protecting him as his eyes flickered and slowly opened. Eriswen looked stunned from the other end of the room. Lyva was nowhere to be found, and Kyren sighed in silent relief. Reth leaned against the wall beside Nyk's body.

*Nyk... is dead?* Kyren wondered what happened and felt a twinge of sorrow for his old friend.

*"Destruction!"*

Kyren gasped in horror. Destruction was a legendary spell that Mathas had only briefly told them about. No one had ever done it in thousands of years...

It was a spell that killed anyone with magical power.

*"Father, no!"* Kyren screamed. Ignoring the agony breaking through the numbness of his body, he forced himself to his knees.

"Kyren, you shouldn't move! What's going on?" Nassia's eyes met his, frantic.

"Everyone! We have to ban together, using all of our energy at once. It's the only chance we have!" Kyren's voice rose over the noise, reaching every living Magi. Somehow, Boli had freed himself and stood in the room with them.

Reth stumbled over, wrenching Kyren to his feet. "I got you, buddy."

Mordzar clutched Eris' hand, and they held each other up.

Boli wrapped his arms around Dyrdra, while Jesyth grabbed Dyrdra's other hand. He nodded once. Lyva stood in the doorway, and he motioned her over. Even the magical energy of his daughter would help them. If the spell was enacted, Rya would die too, no matter what room she was in.

Nassia stared at them, unsure of what to do. Kyren motioned her over as well. Kyren used his left hand to grab her so that she stood in between him and Jesyth as the other Magi joined the circle. "Shield!" Kyren screamed. His voice was joined by the other Magi, even little Nassia.

Kyren's dark shield formed first, joining together by a darkness-resistant shield Reth had conjured. Eris formed the largest shield, wrapping it around all of them. Nassia's tiny one formed out of pure energy, quickly joined by Enya's shield of wind. Lyva's shield formed in the shape of an energy wolf in the shape of her dead sister. Mordzar created a metal shield and grew it as large as he could. Zentra's shield was like Nassia's, made from pure magical energy. Kanir's energy shimmered and flickered with stoic lightning. Boli's shield was blue in color. Eiridan's mixed with them, enveloping and healing them, as it protected them. Jaeyria's was thick with shadows that danced around them. Jesyth's invisible force of gravity pushed all of their shields outward, covering all the Magi and merging all the shields together.

The shields pressed against Vaxon's spell and all was as it should be; the Magi against Vaxon. Finally, they stood together as one against Vaxon's tyranny. Each one of them had lost someone precious, and those lost loved ones added to the power of their bond as Magi.

Those loved ones appeared behind each of the Magi who had lost them, all made from pure energy.

A man and woman clutched hands as they stood behind Jaeyria, and on the other side of them were Eiridan's parents. Cathri stood behind Kanir, flickering in the flames that created her. Nyk stood behind Reth, who grinned and laughed. Both of them were joined by a third man, one Kyren knew as their other brother. Mordzar's parents and sister stood behind him, and they all looked proud. A large dragon appeared behind Eris as tears brimmed in her eyes. He breathed out energy, adding to the shield, before he was joined by a female dragon and several younglings.

Ren bounced over to Kyren, grinning. *"Papa!"* he shouted and he jumped in his father's arms. Ashyra was right behind him, and pressed her lips to his.

# DARK MAGI

It was a kiss like breathing after drowning; the first gulp of precious air.

In the center of them all, was Mathas. He shimmered in pure white energy, as he raised his hands and strengthened their shield with his own power. Behind him were the faces of many that Kyren didn't recognize—all the Ancient Magi before them. One had red-gold eyes, clutching the hand of a woman beside him. Another was wrapped in robes of an Ancient Magi as he held the waist of a young woman from behind. Another's eyes were blackened, with an air of darkness around him, but he stood beside a woman who was tan with short brown hair. Another woman wore a *katana* on her hip, and she stood beside a man who wore the same. Behind them stood a figure, one that had bat-like leathery wings. Another man held a hand over a woman's pregnant stomach and she smiled warmly. They all stood on a pirate ship, one that held the name *The Liberty Valiant* on the side. At the ship's wheel stood the ship's captain, joined by a young woman with fiery red hair. The man in the Magi robes stood beside Mathas, clapping him on the back. Another man appeared on Mathas' other side, one who looked like just him.

# JOANNA WHITE

In the center of the ship was another man, one who looked young, but appeared wise. He had an air of timeless around him, and gazing on him brought Kyren the strangest sense of warmth and peace. The Father's Presence radiated from the man and Kyren shed tears of happiness and joy.

The timeless, peaceful man raised his hands, and they all joined him, throwing energy into the Magi's shield.

Together, they sent all their energy, all their hearts and souls into protecting each other from Vaxon's attack.

A wild explosion reverberated around the entire area, completely destroying the throne room and Vaxon's entire castle.

*\*\*\**

EVEN FROM THE battlefield, one could see the blast of a kaleidoscope of colors erupting from the castle. It detonated across all of Komesten, forcing soldiers to their knees, good and evil alike. Even the giant dramon and mammoths fell to the ground, shaking the earth violently. Griffins, phoenixes, dragons, and fairies were forced from the skies, as goblins and ogres burrowed deep underground, trying to escape it.

# DARK MAGI

A cold, resounding silence consumed all of Castre that night, and all was still.

## EPILOGUE

THE ENTIRE WORLD pointed to the Father and how He had created it. It was beautiful, reflecting the Father through the stars and feeling His Presence through the wind. From the mountains, birds, trees, to the people and the love they shared for each other…Everything in the entire universe was a painted picture in a kaleidoscope of colors, a song that drummed within the hearts of all people. Good, evil, life, death, day, night, sun and rain… All of it was as it should be and the Father led, controlled, and guided it all.

Death… So many deaths that Kyren had witnessed and even more that he himself had committed. They weighed upon him now, flashing through his mind like a river, one that flowed and twisted around every bend. Each death was a scar, one that was etched into his soul forever.

# DARK MAGI

*Korrah and Kassan, Kyren's closest siblings.*

*Mathas. Executed at the hands of his own son.*

*Dryst and his brother Daek.*

*Kyren's half-brother Keldyr, slain by his own hands.*

*Faeva and her unborn child.*

*Kyren's best friends, Reth and Nyk.*

*Evon and his sister Ashni.*

*Jahad, the uncle who had always been there for him.*

*Ashyra, the love of his life.*

*Ren, his precious little boy.*

*Vassti, his mother.*

All the good that had so many times been squelched by darkness and evil, good that the Magi had so desperately tried to bring back into a broken world seemed so distant at times, beneath all the darkness and pain and death and sorrow.

Evil had reigned for so long, that no one, not even the kingdom itself seemed to be able to recover. It had left a stain upon the world, one that only the Father's Light and His Son's redemption could completely wash away.

Kyren's life had been enveloped in that evil, and his own soul had been wrapped up in darkness. Night had ruled Kyren's entire life, and now, as he stood in front of the grave of his own grandfather and mentor, Kyren dared to hope that dawn was approaching.

MATHAS, BELOVED MENTOR AND FATHER, the gravestone read.

Kyren swallowed back a lump in his throat, as Mathas' voice reached his ears. *"Kyren, one day, you will teach other Magi what I have taught you. You will be a leader one day; a king with thousands of lives looking and depending on you. I won't always be there to guide you, but as you continue believing in yourself, and trusting in all that I have taught you and letting the Father and His Light guide you, you will succeed."*

When Kyren thought back to the man he used to be, guilt reached out with invisible hands and grasped his heart. It twisted and yanked at him, suffocating and choking him. He could not look at his own reflection without wincing. There were times when he wondered who he was, times when he dwelled on failing everyone from his family in the past to his family now. For so long, he had hidden himself away, terrified that those closest to him would leave or shun him for all he had done.

Rain sprinkled onto his hair, dripping onto his lashes like tears. They rippled into a puddle at the base of Mathas' grave. Kyren

# DARK MAGI

stared into his reflection, broken from the ripples, just like his soul that was shattered from all he had experienced. *Who am I?* Kyren's icy blue eyes stared back at himself, and he had no idea who was in the eyes that stared back at him.

At times like these, his mind felt as if it was fragmented—as if all the tragedies, torment, and darkness he had endured for so long had finally won, as if they had finally driven him mad. Maybe so.

Kyren didn't know anymore.

The wind blew, whispering through the trees of the surrounding forest. Kyren gazed out at the horizon of the setting sun that pushed through the gray clouds of rain. For so long, his life had been gray, like the storm, in a never ending cycle of flooding, storms, hardship and pain. Yet the sun broke through the clouds, shining light onto the world below. Orange, red, and yellow were painted across the sky like a great wildfire, slowly being consumed by the dark blues and blacks of night. The moon settled overhead, casting a silver hue onto the world below, bleeding it of all color. Stars twinkled overhead, the only witnesses to Kyren's silent mourning.

Guilt still plagued him after all these years but Kyren knew that Ashyra wouldn't want him to live in darkness any longer. For her, for Ren, and for Rya and the Father, Kyren chose today to live. To find his redemption with the Father guiding him, save others from evil people who would harm them, to make sure no one had to face or do what Kyren did.

Just like the sun's light peeking through the stormy clouds, in Kyren's life, the Father's light reached down to him and taught him that redemption was possible. Every day, Kyren found himself at the Temple, praying to the Father. For many months, he expected no answer, no light, nothing from the Father he had failed so much, from the beliefs he had abandoned, because of the atrocities he had committed.

*"I love you, Kyren,"* the Son whispered to him one day. *"I love you and I gave my life for you, for the sins I knew you would commit. There is nothing you can do that I cannot and have not already forgiven you for. All you need do is ask, my child."*

*"Forgive me,"* Kyren begged as he *fell down on his face in the Temple, sobbing. "Forgive me, Father. Forgive me for the evil things I have done. Cleanse me. Help me to become a good man, if—if that's possible. Let—let me become the father that Rya needs"*

*The Father's presence overwhelmed him and light flashed all around him. In that moment, he had felt a peace unlike anything he had ever known. For the first time in his entire life, Kyren Asherex felt truly happy and at peace, and had hope for his future and for the rest of his life.*

Was redemption possible? It was a question Kyren had asked himself for years, ever since he was a child. He'd asked it about his father for the horrible abuse and torture he had done to him, had asked it about his mother and the way she had mentally tormented him, and then every day after the Magi Wars, he had asked that question about himself. Once, he had no answer to it, but the Father had given him an answer.

Yes. Redemption was possible and it was Kyren's the moment he asked for it and felt it inside his heart. He wanted to change, wanted to be a better man and longed to rise above his past and the grief and the pain and all the horrible things he had seen and done. Kyren wanted to rebuild Castre, establish a Magi Council, help all the races learn to work together and give the people what they needed.

Vaxon had destroyed so many lives and many more had suffered at his evil hands. Kyren didn't feel he deserved to be king, nor did he want it. Instead, he chose to help those that he could, to save people, to restore the kingdom in the months following the war.

He wanted to become a good father to Rya, to give her something he had never been given himself. Kyren even chose to try to help Nassia, who had been so hurt and changed by the events that had happened that she was a completely different girl—no, a woman.

The Republic sent several Magi Guilds to help Castre rebuild and restore itself after what Vaxon had done. The rebels were destroyed, the city and its people saved, and the races all met to try to come to an agreement. Kyren's Magi friends chose to stay on Castre and work together with the other race's representatives to rule Castre together, ensuring no sadistic dictator like Vaxon would ever rise to power again.

Now he decided that he would no longer be the Dark Magi he had once been .That man was gone and the Father had given him a new life and a second chance at life and happiness. Kyren would live life to the fullest. For Ashyra. For Ren. For Rya. For the Father.

For all the ones he had lost.

For the new man he had become.

# DARK MAGI

## SNEAK PEEK AT LIGHT MAGI, REPUBLIC CHRONICLES BOOK ONE

RAGGED BREATHS ESCAPED from the dragon's unconscious body. The massive, ancient creature barely clung to life and it was quite the pitiful sight. Once, this creature had been so powerful—the apex predator of his time. This dragon not only had been one of the Ancient Dragons—the mightiest dragons known to man—but had also been a Black Dragon.

Black—an expert in dark magic.

Now, the dying creature was nothing more than a sack of meat that could scarcely sustain itself. Pathetic. Disgraceful. *Weak.*

A man wrapped in a tattered cloak stumbled inside the cave where the Black Dragon had hidden himself to die. The man hated—no, he utterly despised—how he unwillingly sympathized with the dragon's predicament. His body ached in places that hadn't felt pain in years and, for the first time in almost two decades, he had fought so hard that he had completely run out of Mathanos—magic energy. The battle against the traitors had left him weakened and drained. Once, he had been like this dragon; so powerful that no one could resist him. The Apex predator of his own time. Now, the man was worthless and had lost... everything.

His kingdom. His army. His power. And almost his own life.

Still, the man was stubborn and refused to give up. If anything, knowing that those pathetic children had defeated him, in the end, only fueled his desire to reign again.

Like a phoenix, Vaxon Asherex would again rise from the ashes of his defeat and burn his enemies until they were no more.

He placed a hand on the Black Dragon's head and hesitated. "Odavaii," he whispered. For once, his voice held reverence and respect, but not remorse. Never that; for there was none inside him. None at all.

The dragon growled, but was too weak to even utter a breath of fire at him.

# DARK MAGI

Vaxon collapsed to his knees with a rumble deep in his chest—as close to a groan as he would allow himself to make. Reaching inside his torn cloak, he pulled out a cracked necklace. "This... you filled it with your power and used it to save my son."

Odavaii growled, but Vaxon did not care. After the dragon had flown out the arena, Vaxon had hit him with a powerful spell that slashed his entire underside. It was a miracle the dragon had survived this long, but still, Odavaii was ancient and powerful and clung to life regardless. Yet, despite the creature's massive injury, he managed a warning, this time in the language of the dragons. *"Hai aloor rovirlaan ak Luhaar kol. Sii sar uvak."*

*You cannot destroy the magical necklace. It is empty.*

Vaxon smirked at him, shaking his head as he clenched the magical necklace inside his hands. It was true, that when he struck Odavaii, the power within the necklace fled. He had partially been trying to stop Odavaii and also trying to stop his son from channeling the dark power as well. All of Odavaii's power had returned to him, but now that Vaxon had the necklace, he could use a dark spell, one that could only be cast when Odavaii was injured.

Unlike the other magical creatures in the arena, Vaxon hadn't brought Odavaii there. He had already been inside the cave, so all Vaxon did was simply trap him there. When Kyren had shown up and formed an alliance with the Black Dragon, it had given him a chance to escape.

Fortunately, Kyren's little alliance only further served Vaxon's goals. With Odavaii leaving his cave and his power transferred to Kyren, it allowed Vaxon the chance he needed to gain the upper hand and wound the dragon.

With Odavaii wounded…

Vaxon could cast the spell. *"Merge!"* It was the most powerful dark spell he had ever learned, strictly forbidden from the Magi and the Republic.

To fuel the spell, Vaxon had managed to take his chest full of Mathano stones that he had collected over the years, just before he had been forced to flee the palace. The stones would give him the Mathanos he needed to cast the spell, since his own reserves had run dry after the vicious battle at the palace.

Odavaii roared in agony, the same agony that Vaxon felt coursing through his entire body. Instead of crying out in pain, Vaxon laughed wildly and wickedly. He

# DARK MAGI

may have lost Castre, but the Republic and the Magi would soon be his.

As his body and power merged completely with Odavaii, Vaxon relished in the revenge that would soon be his.

# JOANNA WHITE

## AUTHOR'S NOTE

THERE IS A lot of darkness in Dark Magi, from the use of dark magic, to the evil things Vaxon does, as well as the evil deeds he forces Kyren to do. Sometimes, I look at the world, watch the news, or get on social media, and all I see is darkness and evil. It reminds me that we live in a sin, fallen, evil world.

Through all of that, I have hope. Hope in Jesus Christ and in God and His radiant, unconditional love. It is He who gives us life and purpose and without Him, there is no meaning to life.

I understand that some of you may not like Kyren or the things he does. He isn't a typical hero who saves the day. It takes most of the book for him to even think about doing the right thing. But I love him and the reason why is because he is me.

He is you.

# DARK MAGI

He is all of us.

Most people think or assume they're a good person but the hard truth is that we are all sinners. No matter what you have done whether it's something as simple as gossiping or telling a white lie, all the way to murder, it's still sin against God, our Creator who is most righteous and holy. In the Bible, it says that looking with lust is adultery and being angry at someone is like murdering them.

How many people, then, have I murdered with my anger?

In real life, people don't always make the right choices. We love fictional characters and heroes who overcome all in the end, who triumph over evil, but the fact is that we make mistakes. In Kyren's case, he made a lot of them…

Yet he still came back from them.

But he didn't do it on his own. He did it only by the Father's redemption which represents God's redemption. It's only through Jesus Christ that we can find redemption for our sins, for the mistakes we have made. You and I cannot do it on our own because we aren't the heroes.

Just like Kyren wasn't the hero.

God is.

That's what I want people to take away from *Dark Magi* when they read it.

That God is the hero of every story because He saves us through Jesus Christ. He came down as man, gave His life on the cross, and was resurrected for our sins.

If you would like to know more, please contact me via email at: starwarsFAN316@gmail.com.

*Dark Magi is book one in the Republic Chronicles that will be continued.* It also features a particular scene where the Chosen, characters from my *Valiant Series*, make an appearance. See if you can guess which scene that is.

If you read *Dark Magi,* whether you liked it or not, please leave a review. It helps out authors so much. *Hunter* and *Shifter,* books one and two of the *Valiant Series* are both wherever books are sold. If you want to find out more about my other books, feel free to join my Facebook fan group at: https://www.facebook.com/groups/jwwarrio rs where you will find all the latest info about my WIPs, as well as where you can find the continuation of Kyren's story.

Or visit my website at: authorjoannawhite.com. You can also like my Facebook page at: https://www.facebook.com/authorjoannawhi te.

# DARK MAGI

Thank you so much for reading *Dark Magi.* I hope you enjoyed it and that it made a difference in your life the way it has mine.

*The Republic Chronicles* continues with *Light Magi,* Book One.

Made in the USA
Columbia, SC
21 November 2022